Winner Books are produced by Victor Books and are designed to entertain and instruct young readers in Christian principles. Each book has been approved by specialists in Christian education and children's literature. These books uphold the teachings and principles of the Bible.

Other Winner Books you will enjoy:
Sarah and the Magic Twenty-fifth, by Margaret Epp
Sarah and the Pelican, by Margaret Epp
Sarah and the Lost Friendship, by Margaret Epp
Sarah and the Mystery of the Hidden Boy, by Margaret Epp
Sarah and the Darnley Boys, by Margaret Epp
The Hairy Brown Angel and Other Animal Tails, edited by
    Grace Fox Anderson
The Peanut Butter Hamster and Other Animal Tails, edited by
    Grace Fox Anderson
Danger on the Alaskan Trail (three mysteries)
Gopher Hole Treasure Hunt, by Ralph Bartholomew
Daddy, Come Home, by Irene Aiken
Patches, by Edith Buck
The Taming of Cheetah, by Lee Roddy
Ted and the Secret Club, by Bernard Palmer
The Mystery Man of Horseshoe Bend, by Linda Boorman
The Giant Trunk Mystery, by Linda Boorman
Colby Moves West, by Sharon Miller

Mother of three, a children's worker in her church, and a former public school teacher, LINDA BOORMAN has shared stories with children for 20 years. Now she is writing her own, and her unusual sense of humor makes her stories delightful.

Mrs. Boorman lives in Frenchtown, Montana. She is a graduate of Multnomah School of the Bible and received her B.S. in Education from Eastern Oregon State College. Her earlier years were spent near small Oregon towns similar to the fictitious Horsehose Bend of this novel, her third book.

The Drugstore Bandit of Horseshoe Bend

Linda Boorman

illustrated by
MARILEE HARRALD

A WINNER BOOK

VICTOR BOOKS

a division of SP Publications, Inc.
WHEATON, ILLINOIS 60187

Offices also in Fullerton, California • Whitby, Ontario, Canada • Amersham-on-the-Hill, Bucks, England

Other books in the Horseshoe Bend Mystery Series:
   The Mystery Man of Horseshoe Bend
   The Giant Trunk Mystery

All Scripture quotations are from the King James Version.

Library of Congress Catalog Card Number: 81-84125
ISBN: 0-88207-492-X

VICTOR BOOKS
A division of SP Publications, Inc.
P. O. Box 1825, Wheaton, Ill. 60187

Contents

1 Professor Van Snoozle   7
2 An Easy Sale   20
3 Burglar in the Drugstore   30
4 Another Robbery   42
5 The Thief Escapes   54
6 The Professor Is Jailed   65
7 A Visit to the Jail   73
8 Miss Eva's Hanky   82
9 The Thief Confesses   95
10 "Buttered Bread"   108
   Life in 1898   116

1
Professor Van Snoozle

It was a pleasant August evening in 1898. I skipped down the back steps unmindful of the bowl I carried. Aunt Minnie's chicken soup slopped around inside. Fortunately, only a dab dribbled from under the lid.

Before I reached the edge of the yard, Aunt Minnie stuck her head out the back door and yelled, "And, it's you, Susie Conroy, that best be getting out to Johnson's and back here double-quick." She let the screen door shut before adding, "Sure and do ask about Mr. Johnson's lumbago*, though."

---

*You can find an explanation of the starred words under Life in 1898 on pages 116-119.

"I will, Aunt Minnie," I hollered back.

And I did mean to hurry back. But how was I to know that a Professor Van Snoozle was camped on the other side of the bridge crossing Muddy Creek. And that meeting up with him would take more than double-quick time.

At the edge of the yard I whistled for our old bird dog, Sniffer. Since he didn't come loping up I figured he was jackrabbit hunting. The high desert around our little town of Horseshoe Bend*, Oregon is thick with them.

I'd just gotten to the bridge when I decided Sniffer wasn't rabbit hunting. His painful howls and yelps split the air. It sounded like the Indians were scalping him on the other side of Muddy Creek.

I sped off, with the soup sloshing in every direction.

Across the bridge and at the edge of the road a man sat on a rock with Sniffer's head wedged between his knees.

Before I had time to rush up and break the soup bowl across his head, I came to my senses.

Sniffer had met up with a porcupine*.

I'd watched Papa holding his head that way before. Using tweezers he'd yank those barbed porcupine quills out of Sniffer's nose. The process was agonizing for both man and dog. But if they were left in, the animal would suffer a terrible death.

The man was working so hard on his nasty job that he didn't know I was nearby. I watched as he carefully pinched a quill. Then he pulled it out as fast as greased lightning. He knew the importance of speeding those tearing barbs through the tender nose. All the while he murmured soothingly to Sniffer and lovingly answered every howl.

I couldn't tell much about the man himself. The top of his hairless head was about all that could be seen as he hunched over our dog. I did notice a covered wagon parked beside him and a bony horse cropping grass along the road. It looked as though Sniffer's rescuer was camping here beside Muddy Creek.

I'd about decided to let him know I was around, when he straightened up and grabbing a can of salve, told Sniffer, "Now my good man, I shall apply a small amount of this miraculous healing balm and you shall soon be as good as new. But from this day hence, promise me that you shall not become sociable with any more barbed beasts."

As soon as he'd released him, Sniffer rubbed and pawed his nose, then came whining to me.

The man stood up and seeing me, remarked, "Good day, Madam, this splendid beast seems to be acquainted with you."

"Yes, he's our dog. Thanks for being so good to him," I replied as I stared at the shabby little man standing in front of me. It looked as though all the hair from the top of his head had slid down with a black glob landing above each eye and the rest on his chin.

"It was my pleasure. And now may I introduce myself?" he asked.

Without waiting for a reply, he gave a little bow and continued, "Professor Van Snoozle, the discoverer of numerous unctions* necessary for the welfare of mankind and, er, dogkind."

I wasn't sure what he was talking about, but I decided right then and there, that Professor Van Snoozle was worth getting to know. Not only was he kindhearted, he was a real curiosity.

"I'm pleased to know you. I'm Susie Conroy and I live in the first house to the right after you cross the bridge into town. See the top of that big two-story house over there," I said, pointing across Muddy Creek. "That's ours. It's called the parsonage*, because Papa's the preacher in that church you can see sitting next to our house."

He hopped up on the rock where he'd been sitting. Putting one hand inside his frazzled black vest, he asked, "Aha, and do all the occupants of that fair home have such flaming red tresses?"

Guessing he meant my hair, since it's red, I told him, "Seven out of the nine of us do. We take after Papa's side of the family. That means red hair, freckled faces, and big bones. Only my married sister, Sarah, looks like Mama. Small, dark, and dainty with a creamy complexion."

"Do I detect a sigh there, Madam?" he asked me.

Then remaining on the rock he flung out his hand, lifted his bushy eyebrows and declared, "I am the sole possessor of the Princess Tonic Hair Restorer."

He paused, looked at me and added, "It performs equally well on red and raven hair."

After telling me this he raised his voice again and stared off somewhere past me. "Are you troubled by an itchy scalp? Is your hair thin or falling out? Princess Tonic Hair Restorer will renew its health. It arrests falling hair and feeds and nourishes the roots. You will be amazed at how full and luxurious your hair will become after using only one bottle of Princess Tonic Hair Restorer."

Stopping abruptly, he patted his bald head, then continued, "You are puzzled as to why this marvelous, world-renown discovery hasn't produced hair on my pate*. Madam, the discovery came too late, too late."

He sounded so sad I nearly cried.

But then he perked up and informed me that, "You

must have at least two hairs or it cannot function. Most of the populace can boast of two hairs, thus . . ."

He stopped in mid-sentence when a woman's voice called from the covered wagon. "Professor, Professor, I need you."

The Professor immediately leapt from the rock and answered, "Coming, Princess Falling Mane."

Then he turned toward me, and with his face fallen into sad lines, explained, "That is my good wife, the Princess of an Apache Indian tribe. Her lovely, black hair flows to her feet. It is from her tribe that I gleaned the secrets of restoring hair. You've never beheld a baldheaded Indian, have you?"

"Well, no," I said in answer to his question.

"And now," he sighed, "she is weak and ailing. Alas, I have not the means to purchase so much as a proper meal for her."

"You mean you're out of money?" I asked.

"Yes, that is the unhappy truth," he told me. "But the aroma from your covered dish convinces me that it contains a potion abounding with restoring powers."

"Oh, this," I said, holding out the long-forgotten dish. "I'm supposed to be taking this to the Johnsons'. They live down the road a piece. Mr. Johnson is laid up with his lumbago. So Aunt Minnie made this chicken soup for him. And I'm going to catch it if I don't hotfoot it out there."

"This Aunt Minnie sounds like a saint," the Professor declared.

"Oh, she's bighearted," I agreed, "and awfully good unless you cross her. Get her Irish* temper up and you'd better clear out of the country. You see, she's Papa's sister who came to live with us over 12 years ago, when my twin brother, Tommy, and I were born."

"Halt!" the Professor commanded, raising his hand and eyebrows. "You need say no more concerning this noble member of womankind. I am convinced, that were she here, she would offer this Balm of Gilead* to the ailing Princess without delay."

As he held out his hand, I found myself putting the chicken soup dish in it.

"I'd better get home fast, or Aunt Minnie will have my skin," I mumbled as Sniffer and I turned toward home.

"Give that good lady a hearty thank-you from the Professor and his Princess," Professor Van Snoozle said.

Not waiting to answer, Sniffer and I set off at a dead run. We raced across the bridge and into the yard. Taking the back steps two at a time, I panted into the kitchen, slamming the screen door behind me.

Not till I'd leaned against it to catch my breath, did I notice Mama seated in her rocker by the kichen window. She looked up from her sewing in alarm.

"Why, Susie, is there something the matter?" she asked. "You've banged into the kitchen as though there were wolves at your heels."

"No, Mama," I gasped. "Just that, ah, Aunt Minnie told me to hurry home."

"Well, now and how did you find Mr. Johnson?" Aunt Minnie asked as she hustled into the kitchen. Without waiting for an answer she went on, "Sure and you, Susie, get to stirring up some corn bread for supper. I'm a thinking that will go good with the rest of that chicken soup. If I'll not be missing my guess, your father'll be nigh to starved with him a working in the fields all day."

"Susie, I do think you could hurry without working yourself into such an unladylike dither," Mama scolded. "Now, do tell us how you found the Johnsons."

I plopped down on a kitchen chair and fanned my skirts a bit to cool my legs. Mama looked at me expectantly.

I cleared my throat, then said, "I didn't see the Johnsons." Ignoring Aunt Minnie's surprised snort, I continued, "It's like this, I met a Professor Van Snoozle on the other side of Muddy Creek Bridge. He was pulling porcupine quills out of Sniffer's nose. Anyway, he and his wife are camped there and she's sick. So I gave the soup to them."

Mama's mouth fell into an O, while Aunt Minnie started sputtering, "Begging your pardon," and waving her arms around.

I speeded up my explanation. I told them, in about two breaths, about the Professor's kindness and hair tonic discovery. Before Aunt Minnie exploded, I managed to get in the part about their being poor and hungry.

Mama merely tucked a stray hair into her bun, but Aunt Minnie rammed her hands on her hips and thundered, "And, it's you Susanne Conroy, that best be getting over to that gypsy camp and getting my best covered dish back before that Professor What's-His-Name skedaddles."

"Yes, Aunt Minnie," I meekly agreed.

She didn't hear me for all her muttering. It sounded as though she planned to water the soup down and send Tommy out to the Johnson's next time.

I slipped out the door and ran toward the bridge. Just as I set foot on the bridge planking, I paused. How could I get Aunt Minnie's dish back without seeming rude? They'd hardly had it long enough to finish the soup.

I plodded along to the Professor's wagon still puzzling over the problem. While I stood beside the wagon twisting on a braid, the Professor stuck his head through an opening in the canvas top.

"My, if it isn't my generous young friend," he greeted me.

"Ah, ah yes, well Professor Van Snoozle, my Aunt Minnie, ah, would like her covered dish back," I sputtered, as I felt my face getting hot. "She uses it often."

"But, of course. And I have been thinking about some way by which we could reimburse you for your noble act," the Professor told me as he hopped down from his wagon. "I believe I have the perfect solution. It will reap benefits for both of us."

"Really?" I squeaked.

"Yes, Madam, you shall allow your esteemed friends and neighbors the once-in-a-lifetime privilege of purchasing Princess Tonic Hair Restorer. I in turn shall give you part of the profit from each sale," he told me.

"Do you mean you want me to go to the houses here in Horseshoe Bend and try to sell hair tonic?" I asked.

"But, of course," he answered. "Think of the wealth you could amass."

"I doubt anyone would buy anything more from

Tommy or me," I sighed. "Of course, you wouldn't know, but for the past six months Tommy and I have been selling Mrs. Tidy's Pure Castile Soap. The kind that's pure olive oil with no animal fats added."

"Is that true?" he commented.

"Yes, we earned a coupon for every 12 bars we sold. We finally earned enough for Tommy's box camera*, but we have 88 more coupons to earn in order to get the engraved lady's watch*. And I don't think we can sell another bar. People have gotten so they hide when they see us coming."

"Hmmmm," the Professor murmured.

"Papa says it's no wonder," I continued. "He says if we sold another bar of soap, Horseshoe Bend would suds right up and float off the map."

"A watch?" the Professor questioned.

"Yes, I need a watch in the worst way. I'm always late and behind times. Besides don't you think a watch pinned to a lady's front looks elegant? The booklet says an engraved watch will dress up the oldest calico," I explained.

"But of course," the Professor agreed. "You are to be praised for unselfishly allowing your brother to use the coupons for his camera."

"Oh, no," I hurried to assure him. "We agreed that we needed the camera the most. Tommy has a very scientific mind and we knew he could learn to expose and develop pictures. The booklet said even a dullard could do it."

The Professor stroked an eyebrow and hummed, "Hmmmmm."

"And Abby will need pictures of the family in the worst way," I continued to explain. "She's my next to the oldest sister. She's leaving home soon to go to The Moody Bible Institute in Chicago. She's going to train to be a missionary. Chicago is miles and miles away, so she won't get home for ages."

"But of course," the Professor nodded his head in agreement.

"So, we did need that camera to take pictures of the family to send with her so she won't get so homesick. And then we want one of her, so we won't miss her quite so much," I finished with a gulp.

"Madam, if there was ever a soul who deserved an exquisitely engraved lady's watch it is you," the Professor pronounced.

"I sure want one," I sighed.

The Professor hopped up on the big rock and placed one hand inside his vest. He flung out his other hand, raised his bushy eyebrows and staring off across the way, declared, "Mrs. Tidy's Pure Castile Soap may have cleaned up the bodies of the residents of Horsehoe Bend, but I would hazard a guess that their heads are in a frightful condition.

Many of these citizens suffer from dull and itchy, balding scalps."

He paused, looked at me and added, "They will forever be in your debt if you allow them the privilege of purchasing a bottle of Princess Tonic Hair Restorer. And for you it will mean enough shekels to buy the finest engraved watch available."

Before I could collect my thoughts, I found myself headed toward home with a box of Princess Tonic Hair Restorer. Aunt Minnie's soup dish rested on the top of the box and my brain buzzed with what the Professor called my "sales pitch"*. This included the 101 reasons that every living soul should purchase a bottle of the hair tonic.

As I trudged down the road to the parsonage, I suspected that my family wasn't going to welcome this new selling venture with open arms. However, I hadn't the slightest notion that it was going to involve me in a mysterious robbery.

2
An Easy Sale

I stashed the hair tonic box behind the woodbox on the back porch before stopping in front of the wash bench.

After a hasty wash up, I inspected my hair in the mirror hanging over the bench. A great deal of red hair had escaped my braids and seemed to be dancing for joy all over my head. I wondered if the Professor's hair tonic could help *my* hair. I'd try it when I found time, I decided.

Just as I picked up the comb, I heard the chairs squawking on the kitchen linoleum. The family was sitting down to the supper table. I knew from the past, that being late for supper could result in unpleasant experiences.

I plunged the comb into the wash water and quickly ran it through the front of my hair before scrambling into my place at the table.

Papa glanced at me before he asked the blessing on our watered-down chicken soup. I half-expected him to say something about my afternoon's adventures. But he didn't. He just got right to the business of serving up chicken soup to the eight of us around the table.

At first we Conroys seemed too hungry to talk. Timmy, our baby, slurped his soup right up and Joe, our six-year-old, asked for more in record time.

As soon as possible, I exchanged a look with my twin, Tommy. My look told him that we needed a private talk after supper.

Papa spoke up just as the corn bread platter emptied. "Sure and if that soup didn't fill up my hollow spot, Minnie."

"Well now, if it isn't something of a miracle that Susie left us any," Aunt Minnie told him.

Papa looked at me in surprise. "Begging your pardon. And Susie, have you been up to some shenanigans* again?"

I gulped down the last of my milk before answering. "I shared some of Aunt Minnie's soup with a poor man and his wife who are camped by Muddy Creek Bridge. They didn't have anything to eat. He very kindly pulled quills out of Sniffer's nose too."

"Hump," Aunt Minnie sniffed. "Sure and if he isn't some tramp selling hair tonic."

"Well now, Minnie, we of all people shouldn't be tightfisted," Papa declared. "It's past believing, but Chet Miller handed me this when I left the hay-field to come home this evening. Said to give it to Abby for her schooling."

Papa reached into his pocket and laid a gold piece on the red-checkered tablecloth.

Everyone stared at it, while Papa continued, "And here I'd only gone out to give him a hand, 'cause I knew he was shorthanded and needin' to get his hay in."

"Oh, Papa," Abby squealed. "I've the same kind of surprise." She reached into her dress pocket and placed a smaller gold piece beside Papa's.

"Mrs. Higgins from the hotel gave it to me today," she explained. "I told her this would be the last day I could work for her, since I'll need the rest of the week to get ready to go to Chicago."

"How good the Lord is," Mama chimed in. "Now we'll have plenty for Abby's train fare and enough to see her nicely through the school year."

"God never fails His own," Papa agreed.

"That reminds me of the Scripture in Ecclesiastes

11:1. 'Cast thy bread upon the waters, for thou shalt find it after many days,'" Mama quoted.

She gave Abby's hand a little squeeze before continuing. "Abby has given Mrs. Higgins many hours of extra work. She really ran the whole hotel last March when Mrs. Higgins was laid up. And without any thought of payment."

"She certainly gave me more than my wages were worth," Abby exclaimed.

"Faith and if that don't fit into my way of looking at that Scripture verse," Aunt Minnie spoke up. "Cast thy bread upon the waters for thou shalt find it *buttered* after many days. Whenever we give 'plain bread'—it'll come back to us 'buttered bread.'"

After hearing Aunt Minnie's idea, Papa's laugh bounced off the kitchen walls.

Then he reached over to the sideboard for his big black Bible. "Sure and I'm one man ready to go to bed early tonight. If working in a hayfield from sunup isn't enough to do a man in. Before family prayers we'll look at Proverbs 11:25, 'The liberal [generous] soul shall be made fat; and he that watereth shall be watered also himself.'"

As we prayed around the table, we all remembered to thank God for answering our prayers and giving us enough money to send Abby to the Bible institute.

Papa was scooting his chair from the table, while

covering a big yawn, when Mama exclaimed, "Oh, dear, I nearly forgot to remind you all. Sidney left on this afternoon's stage, so that leaves Sarah alone tonight. Susie, she's planning on you sleeping over with her while he's gone."

"Sure," I gladly agreed. My married sister's husband, Sidney Wright, owned a drugstore a few blocks down from the parsonage. He'd inherited it from his father. His going to a drugstore convention in Portland left Sarah alone in their living quarters over the top of the store.

"Sure and she's apt to be a bit skittish in her condition," Aunt Minnie remarked as she started stacking plates.

"Her condition" meant that she was going to have a baby. In a couple of months I'd be Aunt Susie.

While padding off to bed, Papa yawned and mumbled to himself, "Sure and if Jack Crump isn't running the store. For it's me that's needed out to Miller's on the morrow."

Mama told Timmy and Joe to get their dirty feet to soaking in the washtub. Then she turned to Tommy and me. "You two do the washing up. Aunt Minnie's been on her feet since daylight and Abby and I need to finish her winter coat."

"Mama, I'd like permission to make a visit before going to Sarah's," I said.

"A visit. Where?" Mama asked.

"Just somewhere in town," I hedged.

"Susie, you've been brought up to be kind and generous, so I'll not scold you for sharing Aunt Minnie's soup with that traveling salesman. But, I don't want you visiting that wagon with it fast getting dark," she told me.

"No, Mama, this will be a friend right here in town," I answered. "I'll go right to Sarah's afterward."

"All right, but you be at Sarah's by 8:00. She's planning on you," Mama reminded me.

Tommy and I had our heads together before the family had time to scatter.

"Now, what's up?" Tommy asked eagerly.

"Tommy, I think I'll still be able to buy a lady's watch," I told him.

"Not really!" Tommy exclaimed.

"Yep. That Professor Van Snoozle that I gave Aunt Minnie's soup to, is letting me sell his Princess Tonic Hair restorer. I get to keep part of the money," I explained.

Tommy raised his hand. "Hold it," he said with a serious look on his freckled face. "Remember how we nearly had to beg people to buy Mrs. Tidy's soap. I don't think anyone will buy anything from us again."

I poured boiling water from the teakettle into the

cold water already in the dishpan. Tommy shaved the soap. (It was some of Mrs. Tidy's Pure Castile Soap. We had several boxes left.)

All the time I talked. And while Tommy swished the dishrag over the dishes, I rinsed and wiped them, and talked some more.

I told him how much I needed a watch. I recalled how many hundreds of bars of soap I had sold. Then I reminded him that I'd sold most of the soap that had earned him his camera. (I knew he felt badly about our not having enough coupons for my watch.)

Finally he gave in, "All right, Susie, what's your plan?"

"During supper I decided on our first hair tonic customer," I told him.

"Who?"

"Miss Evangeline Posey," I answered. "Being a boy, you probably haven't noticed, but her hair is mighty thin on top. And you know how she's been sprucing up ever since Jack Crump's been courting her. She's sure to buy a bottle."

So, when we'd stacked the dishes in the cupboard, I grabbed my nightgown from under my pillow. Then after yelling "good-night" to anyone listening, I met Tommy on the back porch. We dug a big, green bottle out of the Professor's box and started off down the main street of Horseshoe Bend.

Miss Eva Posey lived alone in a neat, white house at the end of the street. After threatening to for 20 years, her mother had finally died in March. She'd kept Miss Eva under her thumb all those years, never allowing a man to so much as cast a glance in her direction.

Now, Aunt Minnie said Miss Eva was just like a bird let out of a cage. I agreed. She had Jack Crump courting her regular, while she flitted around giggling and chirping. She'd bought a whole case of Mrs. Tidy's Soap too.

"You do the talking," Tommy said as we opened the gate and entered her clean-swept yard.

She opened the door at the first knock. I figured she thought we were Jack Crump, since he turned in at her gate every evening. No one in town could miss him in that blue-and-white checkered coat he wore (no matter what the weather).

Miss Eva is tall, thin as a rail, and sort of the color of a fragile china plate. Aunt Minnie says she needs to do more eating and less flitting around.

"Hello, Miss Eva," Tommy and I said together.

Tommy must have thought she was expecting Jack too because he added, "Jack will probably be late leaving the drugstore and getting his chores done at home. Sidney left town on the afternoon stage."

Miss Eva giggled and dabbed her hanky* to her lips. "Well of couse. Jack did tell me that . Do come in, children."

"Miss Eva," I piped up. "We've come to share an exciting secret with you."

"Really?" Miss Eva's eyes bulged in her thin pale face.

"Yes. You see, this afternoon I met a Professor Van Snoozle at the edge of town and he told me about this wonderful . . ." I shoved the bottle in her face, "this wonderful Princess Tonic Hair Restorer. It's made up of an old formula from his wife's Indian tribe."

"My, my," Miss Eva exclaimed as she shook her hanky in the air and peered at the label which pictured a lady with lovely long hair.

I continued my sales spiel*, "Your hair will become full and luxurious after using it only a few times and . . ."

"I'll take a bottle," she said interrupting me. "Perhaps I could sprinkle a little on right now, before Jack gets his cow milked."

She glanced up at her clock, then at us, and before we knew it, we were on her front porch, holding the money for the hair tonic.

"Guess Miss Eva means to use that tonic this very minute," I gasped.

"Wow, that was an easy sale. Maybe people are

more worried about their hair than keeping clean with Mrs. Tidy's soap," Tommy reasoned.

I gave a little skip out of the gate. "With sales like this we won't have any trouble at all earning my exquisite lady's watch," I told Tommy.

"No trouble at all," he agreed.

We couldn't have been more wrong. *Trouble* was exactly what Princess Tonic Hair Restorer was about to give us.

3
Burglar in the Drugstore

I told Tommy good-bye at the foot of the steps that go up the side of the drugstore to Sidney and Sarah's door.

Though I was still without a watch, I figured I'd made it to Sarah's by 8:00. I skipped up the steps two at a time, excited about the fast sale we'd made.

Sarah appeared ready for bed when I let myself into their kitchen-sitting room. The dainty, ribbon-tied wrapper she wore set off her delicate beauty. She'd undone her hair and it hung black and shimmering down her back. She wouldn't be a likely hair tonic customer, I decided.

She greeted me with, "Oh, Susie, I'm so glad you came to stay the night with me."

"So am I," I answered, wondering why it was we never got along before she married.

She pushed her hair back and sighed. "I declare, it's so stuffy and hot in these upstairs rooms. It wouldn't surprise me if we had a thunderstorm."

Now that she mentioned it, it did feel warm and stuffy. Sarah had the windows open at both ends of their two rooms, but the curtains hung motionless.

"Listen, I hear thunder off to the west," I said.

"Maybe we'll get some rain from this storm and things will cool off," she said hopefully. We gazed out the bedroom window to look for lightning.

Their bedroom window looked down on Horseshoe Bend's Main Street. Everything seemed quiet and lifeless in town. The hitching posts were empty. Even the Red Dog Saloon appeared deserted.

Sarah said she was exhausted and was going to bed, though she wasn't sure the heat would allow her to sleep.

I took a trip to the little house out back* before getting into my nightgown. On the way down the path, the fresh twilight seemed to have hushed the daytime noises. Coming back, things had picked up though. I heard the thunder rumbles coming closer and a dog yapping from Jack Crump's end of town. I wondered if Miss Eva's hair had impressed him.

Sarah was still awake when I flopped down on my

side of the bed. I told her about the gold pieces we'd gotten for Abby's schooling. I didn't mention anything about the Professor or the hair tonic. Sarah *is not* the type to understand selling enterprises. Trying to earn money for a watch wouldn't be ladylike in her book.

In spite of the heat we both drifted off to sleep. I dreamed of ladies with ankle-length hair, waving big green bottles. They shouted "Princess Tonic Hair Restorer!" as they raised the dust on Main Street. Sarah probably dreamed of cuddly little babies.

We both shot upright in bed, our dreams shattered, when we heard a window-rattling crash beneath us.

Sarah grabbed me and squealed, "Susie, what's that?"

The curtains were flapping in the wind the storm had brought, and lightning seemed to be sizzling all around town. It lighted up the room two counts after the thunder* clapped.

"It must be the storm. Probably knocked something over," I assured her.

"No, the crash I heard was below us. In the store, Susie, in the store!" she cried as she dug her fingers into my arm.

"Calm down, Sarah. I'll go look," I said, as I flipped a leg out of bed.

Her grip on me tightened. "No, you won't, Susie. I won't allow it. No telling what or who's down there. And you're not leaving me alone. Go see if the door is locked."

I found my way to the door during the next lightning flash.

The bolt was undone, so I shoved it firmly into place. Before I had time to take my hand from the knob on the bolt, we heard another crash. It sounded like a lot of glass breaking in the store.

"Susie, get back here!" Sarah commanded.

I ran back to Sarah. "Someone must be in the drugstore!" I exclaimed.

"Of course, there's someone down there. Oh, what will we do?" she cried out as she twisted the bed sheet.

I padded over to the window and looked out. Nobody seemed to be around and the only thing I could hear was the rain splattering on the porch roof beneath me.

I pulled my head back in the window and said, "I'd like to go down and look around."

"NO!" Sarah shrieked at me.

"All right, all right, we'll wait till morning," I agreed. *But in the meantime,* I thought, *I've got to take care of a hysterical mother-to-be.*

I plopped down on the bed and looked at Sarah in

the moonlight. Just like that, the storm had moved farther east toward the mountains. With the clouds gone, the moon shone big and bright through the bedroom window.

"Remember that Bible verse Papa gave Joey when he thought he saw bears in his room at night?" I asked Sarah. "It was, 'He [God] that keepeth thee will not slumber.' It may be night, but God's not asleep and He's keeping care of us," I reminded her.

"Oh, Susie, you're right. I shouldn't have been so silly. But here it is the first night Sidney's gone, and we have someone in the store. Let's just pray and ask God to keep us safe the rest of the night."

We fell into a peaceful sleep almost before the "Amen" was said.

A thumping on the door awakened us. As I slipped into Sarah's wrapper, I realized we'd slept pretty late. We'd been making up for all the sleep we'd lost during the night, I figured.

"Susie!" Sarah called, as I went into the kitchen-sitting room. "Do you think it's safe to answer the door?"

I laughed at her fears. "In Horseshoe Bend, in broad daylight?" I asked, as the knocking got louder.

I slid the bolt back and opened the door. Jack Crump stood on the porch.

He started talking as soon as he saw me. "Mercy on

us, Susie, but I've misplaced the store key and can't unlock the door. Always keep it in my coat pocket, but it's gone," he said as he pulled the pockets of his blue-and-white checkered coat inside out.

"Seems to be," I agreed.

He puckered up his brow and looked so puzzled, I felt like laughing. But I told him, "That's the least of our troubles. Sarah and I heard someone in the store last night. Sounded like they broke something."

"Mercy on us. And here Sidney left me in charge. Oh, my," he moaned as he chewed his lower lip. "And Miss Eva acting so strange. Susie, she had her head tied up in a rag last night. No more than took my coat to hang it up when she gave it back and said her head ached and I'd better leave. Fellow don't know which way to turn."

I thought it was best not to tell him why Miss Eva had wrapped up her head. I did attempt to cheer him up, then Sarah called out to me from the bedroom. I gave him one of Sidney's extra keys and shut the door.

"It was Jack Crump," I explained to Sarah as I went back to the bedroom. "Seems he lost the store key and couldn't open up. I told him we heard someone in the store last night and that really unnerved him."

"Poor Jack. The least little thing flusters him,"

Sarah commented. "But Sidney says he is as faithful as the day is long."

Just then we heard someone pounding up the outside stairs, followed by a bang on the door.

As I started toward the door, Sarah called after me, "Susie, it's really not proper to be answering the door in a wrapper with your hair flying every which way."

Ignoring her advice, I flung open the door. It was Jack Crump looking more upset than ever.

"Susie, Susie," he puffed out. "You're right! There's been somebody in the store! Can't tell if they took nothing or not. But they knocked down that shelf off to the side by the wig display. The one that holds them bottles of cures, tinctures, tonics, and such. Awful mess, awful mess. Better get the sheriff."

"Calm down, Jack," I said as I wondered just how many skitterish people lived in Horseshoe Bend. "I'll come down just as soon as I get dressed."

Jack shuffled down the stairs wringing his hands and muttering something about everything falling apart.

After telling Sarah, I hurried into my clothes. While I twisted my hair into its two braids, I puzzled over the strange happenings in the drugstore.

I could hardly wait to discuss it with Tommy. I figured we could get to the bottom of it sooner than Sheriff Evans. Outside of having a handsome son, I'd never seen that the sheriff had done much for Horseshoe Bend.

Sarah moved at a snail's pace. When she stood up, she complained of feeling faint and sank down on the edge of the bed.

I thought of Aunt Minnie's cure. Hot tea and toast. So before I could get down to the store, I made a fire and boiled the water in the teakettle.

Sarah revived enough to lecture me about receiving guests in my nightclothes and the need for food before beginning the day. Then I remembered it was Sarah's bossy ways that had caused us to squabble before she married.

When I let myself into the drugstore, a strong smell nearly knocked me flat. It was powerful enough to outdo the normal drugstore smells. And flowery-smelling soaps, fishy-smelling cod liver oils, and the bitter odor of medicines aren't anything to sniff at. But this new smell beat them all.

It came from the dark liquid spilled on the floorboards. Jack stood in the midst of the mess, aimlessly stirring bits of glass with his toe.

"Mercy on us!" he exclaimed when he saw me. "Am I glad to see you. Now I can go get Sheriff Evans while you mind the store." He hurried out the door, as though he thought something was about to grab him.

After he left, I knelt down and examined the smashed bottles. The broken shelf had held various cures and tinctures as Jack said. But the bottles I especially noticed were the hair tonic bottles. Maybe it was because I was in the hair tonic selling business, but it seemed to me that the shelf had held mostly hair tonic bottles.

Before I could think about it any further, Sheriff Evans burst through the door, yelling, "Susie, don't touch anything! Leave it be. Leave the evidence to the professionals."

I stepped back and the sheriff wedged his big body into the aisle.

He stared at the mess, then up at the wall where the shelf had been anchored.

"Anything missing?" he asked Jack.

"Mercy on us," Jack sputtered and waved his hands around, "I just don't know. I've looked around and everything seems to be here."

"Hmm," the sheriff mused as he tugged on his chin.

Then he stalked through the store (with Jack and me at his heels) and examined the front and back doors. "No sign of a break-in," he mumbled. "How-some-ever some burglars are clever at forcing and entering."

"Yes, sir," Jack agreed.

We followed the sheriff back to the scene of the crime, where he poked around in the broken glass for a few minutes. His next words left me in a state of shock.

"Just as I figured. Number one suspect is that blathering hair tonic salesman, Professor Van something or other who's camped by Muddy Creek," he declared.

"Is that so?" Jack asked in surprise.

"Yep," the sheriff continued, "can't understand half what that man says, but he's the only stranger in town, far as I know."

"And do you see this?" he asked as he pointed to the label on a broken bottle. "Hair tonic. Somebody was into the hair tonic. It's likely that the Professor's run out of tonic, so he meant to pour some of this into his bottles. Looks like he broke the shelf before he got any."

"But Sheriff Evans, he wouldn't," I blurted out. "His tonic is a special Indian secret and he has some left. He even gave me a box to sell. Besides he's kind. He pulled porcupine quills out of Sniffer's nose, and he's helping me earn a lady's watch."

The sheriff brushed my explanations off. "Susie, you just don't know the criminal type. He's bamboozled you with all those high-falutin' words. Wouldn't trust him if I were you.

"Anyhow, he'll bear watching. He'll slip up and we'll pin it on him, I'm sure," he pronounced as he clapped his hand down on Jack's shoulder.

As he was going out the door, Sheriff Evans called back, "Don't worry none."

But Jack immediately began to worry. "Mercy on us! And with the boss gone and all."

"I'll get the broom and get to work on this mess," I told Jack.

While I swept the broken glass, I thought of ways that I could prove the sheriff wrong. No matter what anyone said, I knew the Professor wouldn't have done this.

There was only one way to free the Professor from being a suspect. I'd have to discover the *real* culprit. And I hadn't the foggiest notion who that might be.

4
Another
Robbery

After I cleaned the floor, I helped Jack repair the broken shelf.

I found myself chomping at the bit, while Jack poked along, whistling through his teeth. He felt the shelf needed to be perfectly square. This took considerable time. Then he plodded to the back room and came back with a box of bottles containing Old Reliable Hair and Whisker Dye. Still whistling some tuneless melody, he arranged 10 bottles in 2 exact rows on the shelf.

Jack now seemed calm enough to carry on by himself, so I told him good-bye and hurried off toward home.

When I reached the back steps, I found Joey and

Timmy playing with some sticks in the dirt. Joey told me Tommy was out in the barn doing chores.

Though I was eager to share the latest events with him, a certain aroma from Aunt Minnie's kitchen drew me through the door.

"Bless me, and if it isn't Susie," Aunt Minnie greeted me. She bent over a large kettle on the stove, forking plump, golden doughnuts from hot grease. The intense heat made her face nearly as red as her hair.

"And it's hungry I 'spects you be," Aunt Minnie guessed. "Knowing the kind of breakfast Sarah serves up."

I sank my teeth into a yummy warm doughnut. "Thanks, Aunt Minnie."

"Well now, and if Sarah hasn't been telling a tale about burglaries in the drugstore. It's past believing," Aunt Minnie exclaimed as she sugared another stack of doughnuts.

"It looks that way. Did Sarah already tell everyone about it?" I asked. I was hoping she hadn't mentioned the sheriff's suspicions about the Professor.

"Well now, most everybody, but your father. That man took himself off to Miller's long before Sarah showed her face around here." She nodded her head toward the front of the house. "Your mama and

Sarah and Abby be working double-time on Abby's school clothes."

Just then Tommy tromped into the kitchen sniffing. "Wow, those smell good, Aunt Minnie."

When he saw me, he added, "Hi, Susie. Heard there was a robbery over at the store."

"Uh-huh," I mumbled around my doughnut.

"Sure and if seeing you two don't remind me," Aunt Minnie declared. "Your Papa left strict orders that you two was to clean the hen house today."

"Oh, no," Tommy and I groaned together.

"Can we wait till afternoon?" I begged. "We've got an awful lot to do this morning."

Aunt Minnie glanced at the clock. "Sure and if the morning don't be half gone. I 'spects you can wait till dinner's over. Well now, grab a handful of doughnuts and skedaddle."

Tommy and I lost no time in obeying. With both hands full we backed through the kitchen door.

After sticking a couple of doughnuts in Joey's and Timmy's outstretched, grubby hands, we headed across the bridge to the Professor's wagon.

On the way I told Tommy about the sheriff's suspicions.

"He could be right, Susie," Tommy commented. "You only met the Professor yesterday."

"I'm positive that Professor Van Snoozle didn't

break into the drugstore and make that big mess. Why would he want that stuff Sidney sells when he has the Apache Indian secret?"

Tommy wrinkled his nose up in thought. "I don't know."

"And, I'm giving all these doughnuts to him and the Princess," I told Tommy. "They're probably hungry."

We found the Professor reclining against his wagon, with his nose in a book.

As soon as he saw us, he leaped up, bowed low, and boomed out, "Welcome to my humble abode."

I shoved the doughnuts in his face and said, "We brought you and the Princess something to eat. How's she feeling?"

"In answer to your kind inquiry, the Princess is still languishing. And your kindness leaves me speechless," he murmured, as he took the doughnuts and attempted to dry his moist eyes on his shirt sleeve. He recovered his power to speak long enough to say, "May the sun always shine on your path."

All his flowery words made me a bit uneasy, so I pointed to Tommy and said, "This is my twin brother, Tommy. He's the one with the mechanical mind."

The Professor stuck out his hand and vigorously shook Tommy's free hand. "It's my extreme pleasure to make your acquaintance. Your charming sibling needn't have revealed your superior intelligence. It is obvious by the elevations on your temple."

"Huh, uh," Tommy sputtered. He looked as confused as I felt.

The Professor carefully placed his doughnuts on the edge of the wagon, wiped his sugary fingers on the seat of his trousers, and thumped Tommy's forehead*.

"Hm, yes, rarely does one find such prominent protrusions," he told Tommy. "You are to be congratulated."

Leaving Tommy with his mouth hanging open, the Professor proceeded to munch on one of Aunt Minnie's doughnuts.

Then I remembered. "Professor, we sold a bottle of Princess Tonic Hair Restorer the first thing last evening."

I dug into my pocket and handed him the money Miss Eva had given us. He separated my share and gave it to me. Then he sniffed, wiped his nose on his sleeve, and snuffled, "May God bless you for your kindness to the sick and the poor."

"We'll try to sell more today," I promised him. "Is the Princess too sick to show us her hair? That way we could tell people we'd seen it firsthand."

"Alas," he exclaimed, as his bushy eyebrows shot up. "This morning she had a most jolting setback. A

47

giant scoundrel, calling himself the sheriff, insisted on searching the premises. Pompous fool. Claimed to be investigating a drugstore robbery."

"I know—it's my brother-in-law's store. Sheriff Evans is all wrong, and I told him so. We mean to prove it, don't we, Tommy?" I declared, as I jabbed him with my elbow.

Tommy still seemed in a daze, but he recovered enough to answer, "Sure, we'll be on the lookout for the *real* robber."

"My champions may be pint-sized, but they are mighty," the Professor thundered as he clutched his tattered vest and gazed at something beyond us.

"Guess we'd better get busy with our selling," Tommy reminded me.

The Professor raised his hand in the air. "Halt—I shall inquire within and see if the Princess can demonstrate what Princess Tonic Hair Restorer is able to accomplish on the human head."

He climbed in the small door and assisted the Princess to the doorway.

This being the first time I'd seen an Indian Princess, I couldn't know what most of them looked like. This one resembled a dried prune. She *did* have long hair. It fell clear to the floor. But the length was the only part of her hair worth bragging about. Her black mane looked like a string floor mop that had seen too many years of work. Of course, I reminded myself, she'd been too ill to use her tonic lately.

The loveliest thing about her was the watch she had pinned to her patched dress. The sun sparkling off its gold case made it look like a rare jewel.

After a toothless smile she turned back into the wagon, dragging her hair behind her.

The Professor hopped out the door and Tommy handed his two doughnuts over. (After all, this was the first person to inform him of his superior intelligence.)

We hurried off so I could continue to earn my lady's watch.

We shared the old Indian secret with six Horseshoe Bend housewives and the old smithy at the blacksmith shop.

Not a one of them could see the need for floor-length hair. None of them claimed to be troubled with itchy scalps or sluggish pores. I knew we might as well give up when we dropped in to see Mrs. Higgins at the hotel. She pulled her hands out of the big lump of dough she was kneading and wiped each pudgy finger on a checkered rag. I handed her one of the large green bottles and she studied the picture on the front.

"Goodness sakes alive, a widder like me don't need hair hangin' down to her knees. Just give me something so's the hair I've got don't look like snow on the roof. Makes me look as old as Methuselah. And me still a young woman" she said peevishly. "I'll just finish up them bars of Mrs. Tidy's Pure Castile Soap before trying something else."

And to top if off, we were late getting home for dinner. I told Mama that a watch could cure my problem of tardiness. And that I was tardy because I was trying to earn a watch to cure my problem.

But my explanations were lost on my family. Tommy and I were sent out to the henhouse with some stern words and hard looks.

Chasing chicken lice and shoveling muck out of a hen house isn't our idea of pleasure on a hot afternoon. So, we hustled through our labors.

Afterward we dived into Muddy Creek. With the help of Mrs. Tidy's Pure Castile Soap we scrubbed away any stray feathers or lice.

For a change, no one could scold us for being late for supper. We arrived early, as clean and slicked-down looking as licked kittens.

Sarah stayed to eat with us and the talk leaned toward Abby's farewell party. Aunt Minnie planned her menu out loud, while Mama fussed about getting the house shipshape. (I didn't like the way she looked at me while she talked.)

It was decided that we had to take the family

pictures as soon as Sidney arrived home. That's when it hit me! By this time next week, Abby's cheerful face would be gone from the circle around the table. I'd miss her like a front tooth.

Papa cleared his throat and changed the subject. "Well now, and what do I be hearing about a robbery, Sarah?"

All angles of the robbery were discussed, but no one mentioned the sheriff's suspicions of the Professor. I breathed a sigh of relief. I didn't want my family to have second thoughts about my friendship with the Professor.

After a lengthy discussion, the family decided Sarah and I would be safe enough in the rooms over the drugstore that night. Sarah said she slept so much better in her own bed, and after all God was with us. (She failed to mention who'd jolted her memory about that fact!)

The next morning when I stepped into the drugstore, I heard Jack bellowing, off-key, in the back room. Something about, "Nobody knows the troubles I've seen."

Ignoring him as best I could, I made my way to the shelf he'd repaired yesterday. There I noticed a white hanky lying on the floor. It was a small lady's hanky edged with several rows of tatting*. A large green smear stained one corner. Quickly I shoved the cloth into my dress pocket and looked at the shelf.

The Old Reliable Hair and Whisker Dye bottles were still lined up neatly. But there were only three bottles in the front row. Two were missing!

"Jack, hey Jack," I yelled toward the back room.

Jack hustled out to where I stood. "Susie, am I glad to see you. Mercy on us, but Miss Eva just isn't herself."

Ignoring Jack's romantic problems, I asked, "Did you sell two bottles of Old Reliable Hair and Whisker Dye yesterday?"

"Why no, I never even sold one bottle. Reason I recall is that Mrs. Higgins was in here just before closing time inspecting them very same bottles. She told me she's chewing over the idea of becoming dark-headed again," Jack said as he scratched his head and stared at the shelf.

Then, he threw his hands in the air and wailed, "Everything's gone wrong! We've had another burglary and Miss Eva barely stuck her nose out of the door last night. She says the wedding's called off!"

"Calm down, Jack. She might change her mind," I soothed, as I stroked the long hair of the wig that rested on a wooden stand.

"Ohhh," Jack groaned.

"Let's not tell the sheriff about this stealing," I

said, changing the subject. "I think Tommy and I can figure it out."

"NOT TELL THE SHERIFF!" Jack roared. "Mercy on us, of course we'll tell the sheriff. Sidney left me in charge and I mean to do things right. We need the law after that thief. I'm going after the sheriff right now."

Sheriff Evans ambled in about an hour later, chewing on a toothpick and looking thoughtful. He poked around for a while, then told Jack, "That Professor must have decided to throw a little hair dye in his hair tonic bottles. Can't figure out how he's getting in here. No sign of a break-in."

"Mercy on us, maybe he got my key somehow," Jack exclaimed. "I lost it the night before last."

"Why didn't you say something?" the sheriff asked as he slapped Jack on the back. "I'll hightail it right out to that Professor's wagon and make a fine-combed search for that key. Knew I'd catch him yet."

After the sheriff banged out the door, Jack went back to singing about his troubles.

I stood by the front window of the drugstore and pulled the hanky from my pocket. *Do Indian Princesses use tatted hankies?* I wondered. I sure hoped not.

5
The Thief Escapes

Tommy popped in soon after the sheriff left. Helping hands were needed at home. Mine to be exact.

On our way home, I told Tommy about the missing hair dye. Then I showed him the hanky I'd found.

While he sniffed at the green stain, I asked, "Do you suppose it could belong to the Princess?"

"It could," he agreed.

We hopped off the boardwalk in front of the Mercantile Store. The dust in the street poofed up around our ankles. "I'll just ask her if she lost a hanky," I said. "But I'm sure the Professor and Princess are innocent. I can feel it in my bones."

"You'll need more proof than a feeling in your bones, Susie," Tommy reminded me.

"Well, it could be Mrs. Higgins. Jack said she was looking at the dye and thinking about using some on her hair."

"Mrs. Higgins?" Tommy asked in surprise. "That's pretty farfetched."

"Do you have a better idea?"

"No," Tommy admitted.

"We'll go see the Professor and Princess as soon as Mama and Aunt Minnie are finished with us," I decided.

Aunt Minnie pounced on us the minute we stepped into the kitchen. Tommy was sent to begin pumping the gallons of water needed for Mama's cleaning. It's a wonder the well didn't go dry.

My first task was floor scrubbing. Then, after getting a crick in my back and raw patches on my knees, Mama set Tommy and me to packing rugs to the clothesline. After that, we worked ourselves into a lather beating them with brooms.

Of course, we weren't the only ones toiling. Mama, her sleeves rolled up and armed with old rags, attacked the dust balls and spiderwebs. Meanwhile, Aunt Minnie flew around the kitchen like ashes from an explosion. Even Joe, looking like a thundercloud, was ordered to dust the moldings and window ledges.

While the dust whirled, Abby whipped her needle

in and out on the last of her school clothes.

Papa wandered into the confusion, nearly tripped over a mop bucket, and remembered a call he needed to make at the other end of town.

Along about mid-afternoon the dust settled. Mama collapsed like an empty sack. After serving up cold tea, Aunt Minnie flopped down beside her.

They suggested that Tommy and I have a washoff in Muddy Creek, then rest till suppertime.

Old Sniffer, who went with us to the creek, looked bewildered when we left the water so quickly. But he shook the water from his fur and followed us across the bridge to the Professor's.

No one seemed to be around, so we knocked on the door. We'd almost decided no one was inside, when the Princess peeked out.

"Good afternoon, Princess," Tommy said politely. "How are you?"

"Feeling a bit peaked," she wheezed. "I believe I've gotten a cold on top of everything else. Ahhhh-choo!" And she sneezed into a large, red hanky.

"Princess, did you lose a hanky?" I squeaked.

She puckered her forehead and said, "No, I don't think so. My hankies are so big, it'd be hard to lose one."

I held up the dainty, tatted hanky I'd found that

morning, and asked, "So this one isn't yours?"

She blinked her eyes and squinted. Then she tittered, "Heh, heh, no, I'd never bother with a little scrap like that, heh, heh."

"Of course," Tommy agreed. "We were just checking."

"Is the Professor here?" I asked.

She stiffened. "No, he's selling hair tonic. I'd better get back to bed. Good-bye." And she closed the door.

Tommy and I looked at each other.

"Now I wonder who took some hair dye and left their hanky," Tommy puzzled.

I chewed on the end of my braid and muttered, "Maybe we'll catch them tonight."

"Tonight!" Tommy exclaimed. "What makes you think they'll be back tonight?"

"A criminal always returns to the scene of the crime," I insisted.

Tommy wrinkled his freckled nose and started mumbling. I knew his scientific mind was at work. He talked to himself from the Professor's wagon right up to our back steps.

Then he grabbed my arm and let me in on his plans for catching the robber. "I've been itching to try out the flash lamp* and powder I got with my Gem camera. This is our chance, Susie," he told me.

"How?"

"I'll get my camera all loaded and the flash lamp ready," he said. "Then we'll hide out in the store tonight. When the burglar shows up I'll focus in on him and you can pull the trigger on the flash lamp. After we develop the picture we'll have positive proof. Even the sheriff can't argue with a picture."

"Wow, that sounds great!" I cried as I danced around him.

"Calm down, Susie, we've got to plan this out. First, how are we going to get permission to be in the drugstore in the middle of the night?"

I tugged on a pigtail and thought. "I know. You can tell Papa that you think Sarah and I need a man in the house tonight. After all, there have been robberies the last two nights. You can sleep on the sitting room sofa. Then, after Sarah's asleep, we'll sneak down to the drugstore and be ready for that crook."

Surprisingly, our family took to our plan like a duck to water. Our after-supper Bible reading included Acts 20:35, "And to remember the words of the Lord Jesus, how He said, 'It is more blessed to give than to receive.'" Papa thought Tommy's giving up his comfy bed for a hard sofa fulfilled Jesus' words.

We both squirmed a little when Papa told us this. Knowing we were misleading our family took a big chunk of joy away from our coming adventure. But we collected Tommy's camera equipment and hid it behind the drugstore counter anyway.

Once we were at Sarah's house, it seemed as though she would never go to bed. She stitched primly on baby clothes while Tommy studied his *Scientific American* Magazine. I examined the lady's watches in the Sears and Roebuck Catalog. And fidgeted.

Finally Sarah laid her sewing aside, rubbed her eyes and exclaimed, "Goodness, it's almost 9 o'clock. I'll make up Tommy's bed out here and we'd best turn in."

I stretched out as stiff as a board beside Sarah,. I had to stay awake till Sarah fell asleep. Then I was to let Tommy know.

I opened my eyes as wide as I could and recalled the watches I'd just looked at in the catalog. There must have been 50 watchcase designs. Flowers seemed to be the favorite design. But there had also been stars and stripes, countryside scenes, butterflies, birds, and antlered stag heads. Each scene was surrounded by curlicues and flourishes. If none of these suited a person's fancy, they offered two "insert your own picture in the cover" styles.

I sank farther into the down mattress, relaxed my eyes and imagined myself tucking the picture of the hair tonic robber into the lid of my watch.

Robber! I jerked awake at the thought.

Then I remembered Sarah and peered over toward her side of the bed. A ladylike sigh escaped from her lips. She turned a bit, then continued to breathe evenly.

Cautiously, I swung my legs over the edge of the bed. With the faintest rustle, I wiggled into my clothes, and tiptoed into the other room.

By the snorks and snuffles coming from the sofa, I knew Tommy was fast asleep. But the tap I gave him on his head brought him to life.

He jumped and yelled, "Ow, what's going on?"

"Shhh," I cautioned, "it's me."

He rubbed his eyes, yawned and whispered, "That's right. We'd better get right down to the store. Is Sarah asleep?"

"Yes," I whispered back.

He'd fallen asleep in his clothes. We crept to the door, lifted Sidney's extra key from its nail, and eased out the door. The nearly full moon lit our way as we sneaked down the steps.

"I wonder what time it is?" I murmured. "If I just had a watch . . ."

Tommy whispered, "The Red Dog Saloon seems closed and the moon's pretty high. I'd guess it's around midnight."

Tommy stuck the key in the door. "I hope the burglar hasn't been here and left."

A cold shiver crept down my spine. "Oh, Tommy, what if he's still in there?"

The key scraping in the lock sounded as loud as a pistol shot. We tensed, ready to dash off at the slightest rustle. But there was none.

We slowly pushed the door open and sneaked into the back room of the store. Tommy closed the door without a sound. It was black inside.

"It'll be lighter out in the store," Tommy whispered. "The moon will be shining through the front window. I'll lead the way, you hang on to my shirt."

I grabbed Tommy's shirt and shuffled along as he felt his way through the boxes to the door going into the store.

Tommy was right. The moon shining through the big front window made finding our way easy.

After picking up Tommy's camera and flash lamp, we hid behind the crutches and brace counter. We would be out of sight to anyone coming in the front door, but have a good view of the hair tonic and dye section.

When we'd plopped down on the floor, Tommy held his flash lamp up in the moonlight.

"Now, Susie," he told me. "You have to pull this trigger which strikes the match, which lights the powder. You have to do it the second I tell you. That flash of light has to be at the exact minute that the shutter on the camera opens. Otherwise, there won't be enough light to get a picture of the burglar. And be careful that you don't spill the flash powder off the top of it."

"OK," I agreed. "I'll pull this lever the minute you say."

Tommy carefully leaned the lamp against the bottom shelf of the counter. He picked up his camera. Then we settled down to wait.

At first the silence made my ears ring. After awhile, I picked up a sound here and there. A mouse scratching in the wall, a board creaking, and the steady tick of the clock behind the counter. The drugstore odors made my nose tickle. Then, I noticed how the moonlight falling on everyday articles in the store made eerie shadows. I reached out to touch Tommy.

He was gone!

I nearly panicked before I saw that he had crawled over to the Homeopathic Remedy* display. There he peered through one viewfinder on his camera.

Suddenly he stiffened. My heart skipped a beat. Someone was turning the key in the front door!

For a minute I was paralyzed. Then picking up the flash lamp, I inched my way to Tommy's side.

The hinges squeaked and squeaked as the front door opened and closed. We followed the robber with our ears as he tiptoed across the floor right to the scene of his earlier crimes.

Peeking around the corner of the counter, we waited for the robber to arrive at the hair tonic and dye shelf, so we could take his picture. But he never came into view.

We eased farther around the shelf. It seemed he wasn't going to the hair tonic and dye section after all.

Tommy sped around the corner. I hustled to keep

up with him. Without warning, Tommy stopped dead in his tracks. I didn't. As I rammed into his back my finger hit the lever on Tommy's flash lamp. The blazing powder flared up so brilliantly that it blinded our eyes.

In that instant a feminine voice shrieked, "Eek, ooh!" This was followed by the sound of running feet in the direction of the door.

Before we could collect our thoughts and regain our vision, the door squeaked open and banged shut. Once more we were alone, wrapped in an awful smelling haze that made our eyes water. I looked at Tommy through my tears. "I'm sorry I ruined our picture," I sniffed.

"That's OK," Tommy said as he wiped at his eyes. "It was a good try."

"We know one thing for sure. Our burglar is a woman, and so is Mrs. Higgins," I told Tommy.

"Since we didn't see who it was, we can't be sure it wasn't the Princess," Tommy argued. "So we're no better off than we were before."

6
The Professor Is Jailed

Tommy and I agreed, just before sneaking through Sarah's door, not to breathe a word about the woman in the drugstore.

We didn't need to. The three of us had just gathered around Sarah's table for breakfast, when Jack Crump's banging and yelling at the door lifted us out of our chairs.

"Goodness! What can be wrong with Jack now?" Sarah exclaimed, as she hurried to the door.

When Sarah opened the door, Jack stumbled into the kitchen. He wrung his hands and sputtered, "Mercy on us, but there's been another robbery."

"Another robbery! This is getting ridiculous. The sheriff will just have to spend the night in the store till Sidney gets home," Sarah said grimly.

"I'm sorry about the whole thing, Mrs. Wright," Jack wailed. "It seems everything is falling apart since Sidney left. Miss Eva's determined to put off our wedding date and she's still not letting me in to see her."

Ignoring Jack's broken heart, Sarah asked, "What did they take this time?"

"Mercy on us, they took that Ideal Lady's Wig, that Sidney set such store by," Jack lamented.

"Naturally—that wig was important to him," Sarah snapped. "It cost him a good deal."

"Oh, mercy on us," Jack started moaning again.

Sarah turned to Tommy and me. "You two go down and mind the store, while Jack goes for Sheriff Evans."

The first thing Tommy and I did was examine the scene of the crime. Sure enough, the lady's wooden head, that had displayed Sidney's longest and most luxurious wig, was as bald as an egg.

"And to think we were right here when it happened," Tommy said sadly.

"No wonder she didn't come over to the hair tonic and dye shelf. But how were we to know she was after a wig this time?" I asked.

In no time at all, the sheriff burst through the door and stomped over to the baldheaded wig stand.

"Humph, now we've something to go on," he boomed as he rubbed his hands with satisfaction. "I've solved the mystery, Jack."

"You have?" Jack squeaked in unbelief.

"Yep. I knew all along that that Professor was guilty," the sheriff declared. "He uses that wife of his to exhibit the powers of his hair tonic. 'Tain't natural for a human being to have hair like he claims. So, he stole that beautiful wig for her to wear."

I couldn't be still a minute longer. "No, Sheriff Evans, you're wrong!" I cried. "We saw her floor-length hair ourselves."

The sheriff glowered at me. "Susie, you stay out of the workings of the law. This is official business, nothing for children to get into."

"It'll sure be nice not to have any more robberies," Jack sighed.

"There won't be," Sheriff Evans insistd. "I'll leg it over to the jail and make sure all's ready. Then, I mean to arrest them two and put them behind bars where they belong."

"Tommy, come on," I whispered. "We've got to get out to the Professor's and warn him."

Tommy and I flew down Main Street and out across the bridge as if a posse were after us. By the time we reached the Professor's wagon, I had a pain in my side and my breath was coming in gulps. I supposed my face was as red as Tommy's.

"Professor, Professor," I gasped, while Tommy beat on the door.

The Professor poked his shiny head out the door. He raised his bushy eyebrows and asked, "And to what do we owe the honor of this early morning call?"

I put it to him bluntly. "Professor Van Snoozle, did the Princess happen to go to the drugstore about midnight?"

This time his eyebrows nearly shot off his head. "Madam, my wife is a lady of the highest standing. Perhaps you have forgotten that she is royalty."

"Well we didn't really think she was the one who stole the wig last night," Tommy assured him.

"We know she's innocent," I added, "but the sheriff doesn't."

"And here he comes," Tommy told us.

Sure enough, when the three of us looked toward the bridge, we saw Sheriff Evans pounding across the bridge planks, looking like he meant business.

As soon as he was within hearing distance, the Professor called, "The top of the morning to you, Sheriff Evans."

He then flung the door wide open and gave a little bow.

"I've come to search the premises," the sheriff

stated as he thrust his big body through the door.

Standing on tiptoe, Tommy and I peered through the doorway.

A curtain divided the wagon in two. The sheriff poked around in some boxes, while the Professor slipped behind the curtain.

In a minute he popped out again. "The Princess is now attired. You may impose your humiliating investigation upon your innocent subjects," he told the sheriff.

He pushed the curtain back and we could see the Princess sitting on the edge of the bed, her long hair tucked under her.

The sheriff took a step toward the Princess. "Aha," he exclaimed as he grabbed hold of her hair and pulled it off!

She clapped her hands down on the short, gray stubs which now covered her head. The sheriff promptly stepped to the doorway, holding the wig at arm's length.

"Here's the proof. The stolen wig from the drugstore," he roared, giving the wig a vigorous shake. "I'm going to stick you two behind bars. Tonight, I'll guard the store. If there's no more robberies, it'll prove you two are guilty. Get your things together."

All the time he was barking out orders, he held the

wig like a person would hold a dead cat. He shook it to emphasize his terrible plans. The wig tumbled down into our uplifted faces. A revolting smell oozed from it.

Tommy and I stepped back. "Whew, that thing stinks," Tommy complained.

"It sure does," I agreed. "And it looks like Mama's old mop. That sure isn't Sidney's Ideal Lady's Wig."

Tommy gave me a little shove. "You're brave, Susie, tell the sheriff."

"I will," I sputtered as I moved up to the doorway again. "He can't put those poor, kind people in jail for something they didn't do."

But before I had time to open my mouth, I thought of how unkind it would sound to say that the Princess' wig stunk like a polecat*. And how badly they'd feel when their lying about her hair was brought right out in the open.

While my brain remained in a muddle, the sheriff hustled the Professor and Princess out of their wagon.

The Professor stepped down with dignity. Then he turned to help his wife. He treated her as though she were a crowned princess, instead of an old woman looking like a picked chicken. (In spite of what my booklet said, the gleaming watch pinned to her dress failed to make her look charming.)

The Professor, unlike the sheriff, did not ignore us. "I bid you farewell, my cherished friends," he said as he gave us each a firm handshake.

"We'll be down to see you," I promised.

With the wig tucked under his arm, the sheriff herded them into town. They looked so small and helpless as he hulked along behind them.

"Now we've got to prove they're innocent," I insisted. "We can't leave them behind bars like common criminals."

"But how?" Tommy sighed.

"That's easy. When the real robber shows up tonight, the sheriff will catch her. Then she'll be behind bars and the Professor and Princess will be free."

"I hope you're right," Tommy worried.

7 A Visit to the Jail

Tommy and I trailed along behind the sheriff and his prisoners.

"Now we'll have to sell lots of hair tonic." I sighed.

Tommy kicked a rock in the road and asked, "Why?"

" 'Cause. With the Professor and Princess slapped behind bars, they can't sell any," I reminded him. "And I still need that watch. By the way, what time is it?"

"Yipes! It must be late," Tommy sputtered. "And Mama told us to get home first thing this morning."

Our racing into the yard caused Mama to look up from the curtain she was pinning to the clothesline. Her mouth had a firm look to it.

"Do you two realize the morning's half gone?" she asked grimly.

We hung our heads. "We're sorry Mama, but our friends, the Professor and his wife, have been put in jail," I explained.

She gasped, "Oh dear, whatever have they done?"

I flipped a braid over my shoulder. "They haven't done a thing. But the sheriff ran them in on some flimsy evidence. He thinks they're the drugstore robbers, but they're not," I growled.

"Susie, calm down," Mama advised as she laid her hand on my shoulder. "You look like a bear with a sore paw. Remember, the sheriff knows more about robberies than we do. Perhaps they *are* guilty."

I crossed my arms and maintained, "They aren't. They're kind and generous and the sheriff doesn't know what he's talking about."

Mama put on her "don't argue with me" look and said, "Susie, you *are* to show respect to Horseshoe Bend's keeper of the law. We've known him for years and the Professor is new in town."

I knew better than to continue the discussion. I'd been brought up obeying what the Bible says about respecting authority. But her doubts about my friends only made me more determined to prove them innocent.

However, the rest of the day found us polishing

window glass, instead of tracking down clues to identify the *real* drugstore robber.

Papa barely finished thanking God for our supper that night, when Aunt Minnie burst out with, "'Tis past believing, but if the sheriff don't already have them drugstore robbers caught."

"Well now," Papa said as he forked a slice of bread, "seems that be all over town."

Aunt Minnie looked at me. "Sure and to think that our Susie here, has been befriending them. Even to giving them my soup."

I squirmed a little and looked to Papa to defend me. He did. "Well now, Minnie," he argued. "Sure and if God don't call us to take the Gospel to sinners. And maybe chicken soup too," he added with a wink at me.

Encouraged by Papa's words, I asked, "May I please go down to the jail after supper and cheer them up?"

"Me too," Tommy chimed in.

Mama entered the discussion. "I'm not sure that would be a good idea."

"Well now, if 'twas me being asked," Aunt Minnie declared, "I'd be for saying no. Think of the bad influence them crooks could have on innocent children."

"Sure and if everybody'd give me a chance to get a

word in edgewise," Papa boomed out. " 'Twill do little harm for the twins to be going and visiting that poor man and his wife."

That silenced everyone around the table. But a quick glance at Mama's, Aunt Minnie's and Abby's faces told me that they didn't agree with Papa.

Misery settled in like a toothache. Aunt Minnie's creamy bread pudding might have been clothes' starch, for all I enjoyed it. Having three of my favorite people disapprove of my actions made me heartsick.

Just when I'd decided to leave the Professor and Princess to their fates, a thought popped into my head. Tommy and I were the only ones who could rescue them! No one else cared or knew about the dropped hanky and the smelly wig.

Papa's voice broke into my gloomy thoughts. "Well now, if we be having jail visitations around here, we'd best look into God's Word and see how it's to be done."

I perked up and asked, "Papa, does the Bible really tell about visiting jail?"

Papa took his big, black Bible from the sideboard. As he flipped through the pages he told us, "Sure and it seems these prisoners were innocent. In Acts 16, starting at verse 16 and going through to verse 34, is where it tells the story."

Then Papa read the passage to us. It told all about

Paul and Silas being thrown into jail for no good reason. They spent their time singing praises to God. Then God sent an earthquake to get them loose. In the end, the jailer was saved by believing on the Lord Jesus Christ.

Before we prayed around the table, Papa had us learn verse 31. "Believe on the Lord Jesus Christ, and thou shalt be saved, and thy house."

As Tommy and I were leaving to go to the jail, Papa told us that would be a good verse to tell the Professor and his wife.

We found the Professor and Princess locked securely behind the iron bars that enclose the back corner of the jailhouse. The Princess lay tucked under a blanket on one narrow cot. The Professor sat reading on the other. He glanced up as we slipped through the outside door.

When he realized it was us, he jumped off the bed and stuck his hand through the bars.

"Good-evening, my faithful young friends," he called out as we tiptoed over to the bars and shook his hand.

"Where's Sheriff Evans?" I asked.

"He removed himself to the hotel, so that he might dine," Professor Van Snoozle replied. "He seems confident that these bars won't allow his two notorious thieves to escape." The Professor grabbed

hold of the bars and attempted to shake them.

"I feel terrible about you being in there when Tommy and I know you didn't do a thing," I cried.

"Your sympathetic spirit is much appreciated my dear young lady, but do not waste tears on us," he said.

He flung his hands out through the bars and continued, "First, we are warm and sheltered from the elements. Second, the victuals we were served for our dinner were superior. No doubt these comforts will hasten the Princess' recovery from her infirmities."

"I'm glad to hear that," I said. "And we plan to work

hard on selling tonic and uncovering the real bandit."

"That's right," Tommy agreed. "We have some good clues."

"Maybe the thief will show up again tonight. Sheriff Evans plans to sleep in the store. Then he'll see he's locked up the wrong people!" I exclaimed.

"Ah, the Sheriff of Horseshoe Bend has informed me of his clever plan. But," and the Professor's eyebrows shot up, "he is convinced this will prove we poor, innocent victims are guilty."

That reminded me of the innocent prisoners in the Bible. "Paul and Silas were innocent when they were put in jail too," I said.

The Professor wrinkled his hairless forehead and confessed, "I do not believe I have had the honor of meeting the gentlemen."

"They're two preachers who lived a long time ago. The Bible tells about them," Tommy told him.

"God sent an earthquake, so they could break out of jail," I continued.

"Are you suggesting that as a means of escape?" the Professor asked.

"No," I went on, "but the jailer was scared out of his wits. If a prisoner escaped in those days, the jailer was killed."

Tommy interrupted with, "That's right, so instead

of leaving the jail, Paul told the jailer and his family how to be saved."

"Saved from being killed?" the Professor asked.

"No," I promptly answered. "Saved from his sins so he could meet God with his sins forgiven."

"Paul said, 'Believe on the Lord Jesus Christ and thou shalt be saved and thy house,'" Tommy recited.

"It is a good thing my profession has to do with healing mankind of his numerous diseases and not imprisoning guiltless humans," the Professor declared.

"But everybody's a sinner!" I exclaimed.

The Professor looked down at the floor and tugged on a vest button. Then he muttered, "I assume you are referring to that small falsehood I spread concerning the Princess' hair."

"We've all done wrong things, not just you," Tommy assured him. "That's why Jesus had to die on the cross. He was perfect, so He could pay for the wrong things we do. You just have to ask Him to save you from your sins."

The Professor looked up and said, "Spoken like a true preacher."

Tommy and I weren't sure what to do next, so we slipped a Bible through the bars and headed toward the door.

Before leaving I turned and said, "Be sure and read

that Bible, Professor. And you and the Princess should ask Jesus to be your Saviour."

He clutched the Bible to his chest and called, "May your dreams be sweet my dear friends and may the sheriff apprehend the genuine thief. And I will apply my mind to the words of advice you have given."

Tommy and I were more than ready to go to bed when we arrived at Sarah's upstairs rooms. It had been a long day, following a short night.

I didn't even have enough zip to talk back when Sarah lit into me about how unsuitable it was for a young lady to visit a jail.

I woke only once during the night. The sheriff's loud snork-snorks and guff-guffs filtering through the floorboards brought me out of a deep slumber. *His snoring is enough to scare any thief away,* I thought, as I turned over and snuggled into my pillow.

Evidently it did. The sheriff told Sarah, first thing the next morning, "No need to worry anymore. I knew I'd caught the crooks. We'll keep them locked up till Sidney gets back to town and tells us what he wants done with them."

His words made my back stiffen up. We'd prove him wrong yet.

8
Miss Eva's Hanky

After overhearing the sheriff's lofty announcement to Sarah, we scurried down to the drugstore, hoping to find evidence of another burglary.

But, before the door had time to swing shut behind us, Jack frisked out from the back room, kicking up his heels like a colt in the spring. He whistled some merry little tune, till he saw Tommy and me. Then he called out, "Mercy on us, but everything's in apple-pie order now. Had a cozy little visit with Miss Eva last evening. She's still putting the wedding date off, but she'll come around. Them robbers are locked up, so no more robberies. And I found the key!"

He reached in his pocket and pulled out two keys. "Most peculiar thing. When I reached into my pocket to unlock the door this morning, there were two keys. Sidney's and the one I lost. Most peculiar," Jack repeated as he scratched his head.

"Goes to show the Professor didn't have it," Tommy reasoned.

"Nope. He must've got in some other way," Jack said.

I glanced around the store, then asked Jack, "Are you sure someone didn't get in here last night while the sheriff was asleep?"

"Yep, I'm sure. I've given the place a good going over. It's all ready for Sidney when he gets in on this afternoon's stage," Jack said brightly.

Tommy and I took Jack's word about "no robbers" and left.

Out on the drugstore porch, we slumped down on the bench and leaned against the dusty window molding.

Tommy moaned, "I've got to think on this."

So while Tommy crinkled his face in thought, I talked. "Things look pretty bad for the Professor. As soon as he's locked up, the robberies stop. Of course, Mrs. Higgins would know the sheriff spent the night in the store. He's one of her boarders. So whose hanky was that? Mrs. Higgins'? And do you suppose she has Sidney's Ideal Lady's Wig? And how come the key shows up all of a sudden?" I asked while watching Bud Miller rein his horse into the hitching post.

I looked at Tommy for an answer, but he'd closed his eyes. "I might as well be talking to the porch post. How can we discuss this when I can't even see your eyeballs?" I growled.

Bud Miller clumped up the porch steps and asked, "How are the two carrottops doing this morning?"

I answered for the two of us. "Having trouble."

"That sounds like normal." He chuckled as he went into the store.

After all that brain work, Tommy finally opened his mouth and said, "I can't figure out any way to help the Professor."

"We can at least sell some of his tonic," I told Tommy.

"Not me," Tommy objected. "I'm not cut out for selling. You make the sales and I'll go home and do the chores."

We agreed on this arrangement. So, while Tommy did our work at home, I slipped off with a couple of bottles of Princess Tonic Hair Restorer under each arm.

I'd thought of a new sales pitch to use on some of our church members. I'd throw in a Bible verse. Sarah had used it when she'd scolded me for not brushing my hair 100 strokes every night.

Mrs. Duncan seemed the most likely church member. Papa always described her as a godly woman. I found her sitting on her back steps snapping beans. Her two little girls, Mary and Martha, were playing at her feet. She welcomed me with a big smile.

"Good morning, Mrs. Duncan," I said as I set one bottle on the ground and extended the other one toward her.

Wasting no time on chitchat, I began, "The Bible says a woman's hair is her glory. So I've brought you a special tonic that will make your glory even more glorious. One bottle of Princess Tonic Hair Restorer will make your hair as glorious as the angels! And you wouldn't want Mary and Martha to look drab, either, would you?" I added as an afterthought.

Mrs. Duncan's astonished look gave way to one of amusement. Then she laughed outright and said, "Oh, Susie, I'm sure the Apostle Paul would never recognize his own words."

Feeling a bit miffed, I snapped, "This tonic was made from an Apache Indian secret."

"I wouldn't offend you for the world, Susie," she soothed, "but our glory will just have to remain unglorious, I'm afraid."

Martha, the baby, tottered over to the bottle on the ground and tried to pick it up. She cried when I took it from her. *Seems the only person who wants the tonic is someone without a mite of money,* I thought bitterly as I hiked to the next church member's house.

Though I called on every church attender I could think of, not one felt the glory of their hair needed Princess Tonic Hair Restorer. None of them were led to buy it for their thin-haired husbands or straggly headed children either.

I did make one sale to a churchgoer. Mrs. Clackenbush, who specializes in raising cats, bought a bottle of tonic to use on some cats suffering from mange*. I asked her to let me know if it worked. Maybe I could peddle tonic to animals, since people didn't have enough sense to see its benefits.

By suppertime, I was so down in the mouth, my chin was dragging. Everybody's lively spirits made me feel as though they were laughing at my funeral.

Sidney had come in on the afternoon stage, so he and Sarah had been invited to eat with us. All during supper, Sarah clung to Sidney as though he'd been gone for years. The rest of the family filled him in on all the latest happenings. Of course, that included the drugstore robberies.

"It was so frightening," Sarah shuddered as she clutched Sidney's arm. "To think the store was being robbed directly beneath us."

Sidney smiled at her and patted her hand. "I won't be leaving you again soon. I'm only glad the sheriff has them safely jailed."

"Susie even took soup to them," Joe blurted out.

I felt like stomping on Joe's toe, but instead I stuck my nose in the air, refusing to look ashamed of my actions.

"Well and if it didn't turn out to be nothing but a gadabout peddler," Aunt Minnie declared as she refilled coffee cups.

"They're sure he committed the robberies?" Sidney asked.

"I'm not!" I spit out. "Just wait till you see that wig they're supposed to have stolen from you."

"Susie, that will be enough," Mama said quietly, but firmly.

Papa cleared his throat and asked, "Well and how did the jail visit last evening come off?"

"We gave the Professor the verse, Papa," Tommy said. "And he said he'd think on it. The Princess was sleeping."

"Faith, and there be a princess even!" Aunt Minnie exclaimed. "How and all did she get to be a princess?"

"She's an Apache princess, Aunt Minnie," I answered. "The Professor learned about his special hair tonic from her Indian tribe."

"Sure and it sounds like a lot of blather," Aunt Minnie snorted.

"Well now, Minnie, they do be needing the Gospel, the same as any lost soul," Papa reminded her.

"So can Tommy and I go to see them after supper, Papa?" I asked.

"Well now, that idea seems a good one," Papa approved.

"Papa!" Sarah squeaked in surprise. "Surely you don't mean that! To a jailhouse. And this couple sounds most dishonorable."

"Wist and I be ashamed of the lot of you!" Papa roared as he banged his fist on the table. "When God gives to us He expects us to share with others. And He's given us His Word to share. Sure and I'll be having you remember, that's why Abby here is going to the Bible institute. So's to train to take God's Word to the godless in foreign places. Sure and are we to do any less here in Horseshoe Bend?"

Mama spoke up as soon as Papa bit off his last word. Her tiny voice sounded like an echo of Papa's powerful one, when she said, "You're right, Dear. May we never be selfish with the abundance God has given us."

"Amen," Aunt Minnie declared.

As Tommy and I waited for Aunt Minnie to fill up a basket with food for our jailed friends, Mama reminded us all that the family pictures would be taken tomorrow.

"And Mrs. Higgins offered to operate the camera so Tommy can be in the family picture," Abby told us.

Aunt Minnie jerked up from stowing food in the basket. "Faith and did you ever see what that woman done to her hair? Sure and if it ain't as black as the cook stove."

Tommy and I exchanged glances behind Aunt Minnie's back. Then on our way to the jail, Tommy and I discussed the latest clue—if that's what it was. Mrs. Higgins could have taken the dye bottles to change her hair from white to black, but where was the wig? That question still stumped us.

When we got to the jail, the Professor started to cry when he realized the basket of food was for him and the Princess. He blew his nose, wiped his eyes, and blew his nose again before he could speak. "There are no words in any language to express our feelings of gratitude," he sniffled.

The Princess, perching on her cot, gave a toothless smile of agreement.

"That's all right, Professor," Tommy assured him. "Our whole family wanted to share with you."

The sheriff, who had taken his heels off his desk and sprung to attention when we'd come in, hovered over us. "Don't mean to doubt your word, youngsters, but I'd best search that there basket," he said while lifting Aunt Minnie's tea towel from the top. "Don't want these prisoners receiving any concealed weapons."

He licked his lips when he discovered Aunt Minnie's fried chicken and chocolate fudge cake inside. He pinched off a bit of cake and smacked, "Minnie's cooking does beat all."

I was ready to snatch the basket from him, when he set it down and said it appeared harmless. He then picked out a long key from his belt and opened the door a crack. He was still licking his lips when he handed the basket to the Professor.

"I'm afraid I didn't do much on selling the tonic," I sadly told the Professor. "Here's the money for the one bottle I sold."

The Professor took the money and carefully returned my share. He rubbed his bald head and said, "It appears as though Horseshoe Bend's scalps are already in superior shape. It will be many moons before you lay up enough treasures for your lady's watch. Excuse me a moment."

He set the basket beside the Princess and had a whispered discussion with her. In a second he was back at the bars, with something in his hand.

"The Princess and I wish to present you with this token of our appreciation for all your acts of kindness," he told me, dangling the Princess' shiny gold watch in front of my nose.

I stepped back before my hand had a chance to grab it. "No, I can't take your watch from you," I cried. "It's awfully nice of you, but you might need it sometime," I finished, thinking of how they might need to sell it for food someday.

Not knowing what else to do, I shoved poor Tommy through the door and slammed it behind us so hard the windows rattled.

As soon as we were outside, I stomped my feet and exploded, "It makes me so mad!"

"Susie, don't have a fit," Tommy cautioned.

I relaxed a bit and said, "The Professor is so bighearted—and to think he has to be locked up for something he didn't do."

"He is one nice guy," Tommy agreed. "But I don't think he minds the jail too much."

"If only we could help him," I wished.

Tommy puckered up in thought, "We need to unravel the mystery of who *really* robbed the drugstore."

Before he had time to get taken up in a thinking spell, I said, "I know what I'm going to do. I'm going to try to sell another bottle of hair tonic to Miss Evangeline Posey."

"I suppose we could try," Tommy said doubtfully,

as he followed me down the street toward the Posey house.

"She may have used her first bottle up and the Professor and Princess will need some money when they get out of jail," I reasoned.

The first thing I noticed when Miss Eva answered the door was her hair. The tonic had made it full and luxurious looking. Just like the Professor had said it would. Those Indians knew what they were talking about, all right. I wanted to hustle Miss Eva all over town and show the doubters how Princess Tonic Hair Restorer had turned an old maid's skimpy hair into a silky, abundant mass.

While I stood there in stunned silence, Tommy greeted Miss Eva. Then he poked me to remind me it was time to give our sales pitch.

"Miss Eva," I began. "I see that bottle of hair tonic has done wonders for your hair. Would you like to purchase another. . ."

"Ohhhh," she gasped and clapped her hanky to her mouth. Then without uttering another word she closed the door in our faces.

"What's wrong with her?"

Tommy grabbed my arm and exclaimed, "Susie, did you see that hanky?"

"Not really," I answered.

"The tatting. The tatting looks just like the tatting

on the one you found on the drugstore floor after the second robbery."

"How could that be?" I wondered.

"That's what we need to find out," Tommy declared.

9
The Thief Confesses

We decided Aunt Minnie would be the best one to ask about the tatting on the hanky we'd found.

The opportunity came the next morning while I was helping her in the kitchen. I washed the breakfast dishes, while she put the finishing touches on the goodies for Abby's farewell party.

Before plunging my hands into the hot, sudsy dishwater, I pulled the tatted hanky from my pocket. Holding it up by one corner, I asked, "Aunt Minnie, have you ever seen a hanky like this before?"

Aunt Minnie looked up from frosting a cupcake, wiped her hands on her apron, and took the hanky from me. She spread it out, fingering the tatted edges.

"Well now this tatting be Agnes Posey's work for certain. She always used one particular pattern on her hankies. And it's me that's telling you she gave them to half the town. Mrs. Higgins herself told me she owns half a dozen. Where'd this one show up, I'd like to know."

Instead of answering, I dumped all the eating utensils into the dishpan with a great clatter.

"*Susie*," Aunt Minnie bellowed.

While rattling the spoons, knives, and forks, I mumbled, "In a most unlikely spot."

Then to get Aunt Minnie off the subject, I asked, "Do you think that will be enough cupcakes for tonight's party? Seems like all the church people and half the town will be here."

Aunt Minnie slapped a glob of frosting on a cake and assured me that there'd be enough for "everybody and their dog."

Just then, Tommy lugged the morning's milk in. As soon as he set the pail down, I gave him the "I need to talk to you" look. Leaving the dishes to soak I motioned him to the back porch. Out there we strained the milk. While the milk ran through the straining cloth into the pans, I told him what I'd learned about the hanky. And while we wedged the milk pans into the ice cooler beside the raspberry cream for the party, we plotted.

The plan we decided upon, while our red heads were together, was as dangerous as playing with dynamite. But, we figured it was worth the risk. If our scheme worked, sometime during the party tonight, we'd clear the Professor's and Princess' names once and for all.

We'd no more than finished the early morning chores, than it was time to spruce up in our Sunday go-to-meeting clothes for the picture. Somehow we all managed to arrive at the front steps by 11 o'clock. Sarah and Sidney stepped through the front gate looking like a fashion plate from Godey's Lady's Book.* The rest of us weren't so all-together.

"Dear, your collar is crooked," Mama remarked as she stood on tiptoe and straightened Papa's collar.

"And its you, young man, that had best get over here and get that hair slapped down," Aunt Minnie hollered at Joe who was hanging by his knees from the porch railing. He jumped down at Aunt Minnie's loud command.

"Susie," Abby worried, "do you think my hair will do? After all, I'm to have one picture taken of just me."

I looked at Abby's red hair that she wore braided coronet style around her head. It seemed fine to me, but I was a poor one to ask, judging from what Sarah had to say.

"Susie, did you look in the mirror before coming out here? Your hair positively looks like a scarecrow's," Sarah declared.

Frantically, I slapped at my hair. Having hair flying every-which-way might pass for everyday, but not for a family picture. It was too bad I'd never had the time to try Princess Tonic Hair Restorer on it. (And here I'd only been worried because I didn't have a lady's watch to dress up my Sunday School dress.)

Abby calmed my fears when she said kindly, "Don't worry, Susie, only a few hairs have escaped from your braids."

I gave her a hug, while she attempted to force my hair into place. I wondered for the hundredth time how life would be bearable with Abby gone, when Mrs. Higgins waddled into the yard.

Only Mama's constant teaching on good manners kept us from expressing our opinion on her bottle-colored hair.

I gave Tommy a poke in the ribs when he passed me to pick his camera up from the rocking chair on the porch. He looked a bit desperate, but I knew he'd do his part in our plan.

While the rest of us discussed the proper seating for our picture, Tommy gave Mrs. Higgins lessons on using the camera. Due to the loud Conroy mouths, I was the only one to hear Tommy cry out in an

unnatural voice, "Mrs. Higgins, I think I see a spider on the top of your head!"

She squealed and bent over while Tommy grabbed a good chunk of her hair and gave a hearty yank. This resulted in a shocked silence from Mrs. Higgins and "I beg your pardon," from Tommy. Then looking my direction, he shook his head no.

Thankfully, the solemn occasion of our family picture kept me from dwelling on the fact that the next dangerous move was up to me.

Mrs. Higgins grasped the mysteries of operating the camera about the time we decided on our seating arrangement. Mama, in her light gray silk, was seated in a parlor chair, while the rest of us grouped around her. Papa struck a hand-in-the-suit pose, while the rest of us, except Timmy, stood like wooden soldiers. Since Timmy didn't know the proper stance for pictures, he leaned against Mama.

Mrs. Higgins looked into the viewfinder of Tommy's camera. "Don't move," she cautioned.

We held our breath and stood as still as fence posts, waiting for the shutter to click.

Snap!

Tommy reclaimed his camera and turned over, what he called the negative holder, in preparation for Abby's picture.

After taking Abby's picture, Tommy shut himself and the exposed glass plates, into the closet under the stairs. He shared this dark cubbyhole with an odd assortment of bottles containing developers and fixers. Tommy's other equipment, like his photo paper, contact frame, and kerosene photo lamp, was waiting for him in his darkroom too.

Then, because Tommy has a scientific mind and an instruction booklet, he impressed us with two first-class pictures at dinnertime. We all agreed that photography was a marvel.

Just as the August sun set, people trooped into our front parlor. Mama, Papa, and Abby greeted them at the front door, while Tommy and I ushered them to the chairs set up around the parlor wall. I wore my pink and white checkered gingham dress. It has a row of ball-shaped buttons down the front, which figured into our plan for catching the drugstore thief.

A number of people had going-away gifts for Abby. I jabbed Tommy when we saw Miss Eva press a tatted hanky into Abby's hand. Jack, who was at her elbow, grinned from ear to ear. According to our plan, we seated them in two chairs away from the wall.

When everyone was stuffed into the parlor, Papa opened the little program for Abby. First, Nettie Fisher recited a tear-jerking poem about a beloved daughter being carried away from the bosom of her family. It was enough to make the most coldhearted person weep.

People cheered up when the five-year-old McCall twins warbled *Jesus Loves Even Me*. And Papa and Aunt Minnie settled back with a contented smile while Sidney sang *My Wild Irish Rose*.

The Sunday School superintendent closed the program with a short speech. He told Abby how much her "bright and shining" face would be missed at the organ and by her small Sunday School pupils. She blushingly accepted the *Smith's Bible Dictionary* given to her by the Sunday School.

It wasn't till Aunt Minnie signaled for Tommy and me to come to the kitchen that I remembered the time for putting our plan into action had come. The stage was set. I felt like I'd caught the nervous jitters. But our scheme had to be carried out exactly on schedule or it would flop.

So, while people enjoyed one another's company, Tommy and I wandered among them, serving the lemonade, coffee, and tea. Then I made my way behind the row of chairs set up by the wall. I stopped behind Miss Eva's chair, then leaned over her shoulder and asked if she'd care for more tea.

While she fluttered her slender fingers in the air, I carefully twisted some of her hair around my middle button. Then I straightened up and stepped back. Her wig, clinging to my button, whisked off her head.

"Ooooh, eeeeh!" she shrieked as she twirled around to see where her wig had gone.

As if by command, the chattering ceased. All heads turned toward Miss Eva and all eyes looked in disbelief at her slicked-down, purple hair.

Just as Miss Eva flopped over in a faint, I scurried over to Sidney and dropped the wig into his lap. "Here's the Ideal Lady's Wig that Miss Eva stole from your store," I announced.

Papa jumped up. "Sure and my last dime I'd be giving to know what's going on around here!" he boomed out over the heads of our astonished guests.

103

"Dropping her hanky gave her away," I told Papa.

Papa's voice raised an octave. "And 'twill be you that drops, Susie, if you don't explain yourself!"

My voice shook as I answered him. "You'll have to ask Miss Eva why she stole the wig. We only figured she must have done it, because of the tatting on the hanky she dropped at the store. We thought the burglar could've been Mrs. Higgins, but her hair didn't come off when Tommy pulled it. Besides, Miss Eva's hair filled out so fast after she bought the tonic. And we knew the burglar was a woman," I finished with a gasp.

"Hold it," the sheriff growled as he entered the discussion. "Susie, you and Tommy've been meddling with the law again."

Tommy stepped up beside me. Judging by the reproachful looks on the upturned faces, he was the only friend I had. We might have been thrown to the lions by that accusing crowd, if Miss Eva hadn't begun to moan.

That turned everyone's attention back to her. Jack had his arm around her, while he clucked like a hen with one chick. She lifted her head from his shoulder and declared, "Susie's right—I did it."

"What!" "Not really!" "You don't say!" "Well I never!" bounced around the room.

"Yes, I did," Miss Eva insisted. "When I used that

hair tonic Susie and Tommy sold me, my hair turned green." She clasped her hands to her skinny chest and continued, "Green mind you. I knew Jack would never have a green-haired bride."

"Mercy on us, I wouldn't have minded," Jack assured her.

"Yes, you would have," Miss Eva argued, as she stiffened up and faced him. "So when you came by that evening I took the store key from your pocket."

Jack gasped, "So that's where it went!"

"But, oh my, I tremble to think of all the commotion I caused trying to get some hair dye. I planned to dye my hair back to its normal color without Jack being any the wiser."

"Why, you're the one that broke the shelf!" Sarah exclaimed.

"Yes, I shook for hours afterward," Miss Eva sighed as she faced the party guests. "So I came back the next night and took a couple of bottles of Old Reliable Hair and Whisker Dye. I intended to pay for it privately, Sidney."

"Why mercy on us, we all know you're honest," Jack assured her.

Miss Eva fluttered and flapped, looking like she might take off in flight, while she told her story to about 40 flabbergasted people. (The party had become more exciting than planned.) "But, look, just look what it did. It turned my hair purple. I just couldn't have Jack seeing me like this."

"I'd love you with blue hair," Jack said grimly.

"So that's why I had to take the wig, which I planned to pay Sidney for as soon as I could see him alone. After I got it, I put the store key back in Jack's pocket. Soooo," she sighed like someone who'd just had a great weight removed, "that's how it all happened."

Then she no more than finished, when she burst into tears, sobbing, "I'm so sorry, so sorry."

The room came back to life, while people crowded around Miss Eva and assured her that they understood.

Jack announced that they were getting married within the week. Miss Eva needed someone to look after her.

Now that Tommy and I were off the hook, I realized we had been successful in proving the Professor and Princess innocent. I found the sheriff sitting behind the potted palm and told him, "You'd better let those poor people out of jail now. Maybe they'd like to come to the party too."

"Hold your horses, Susie, they ain't suffering none," he said as he shoveled in another mouthful of raspberry cream.

As it turned out, they preferred to spend the night

in jail. Papa called on them before he went to bed. They told him that they thought they had better put some miles between them and Horseshoe Bend the next day.

10
"Buttered Bread"

The Professor and Princess did leave town early the next morning. I guess they had given up on the residents of Horseshoe Bend seeing the importance of Princess Tonic Hair Restorer.

I hurried to their camping spot before the dew had dried from the bushes along the road. The parsonage was in such a hubbub, that I'd slipped out unnoticed. All the Conroys were hustling around to get Abby ready to leave on the morning stage.

I felt they could do without me. It seemed more important that at least one citizen should be kind enough to tell the Professor and Princess good-bye.

By the time I arrived, their bony, white horse was already hitched to the wagon. The Professor was busy examining one of its hoofs.

"Good morning, Professor Van Snoozle," I called out.

The Professor, who now wore a battered straw hat, let go of the horse's hoof and turned toward me. He lifted his hat and bowed. "The top of the morning to you, my flaming-haired sleuth."

"Well, ah, yes," I stammered.

"We intended to call at your home before leaving Horseshoe Bend. We owe our freedom to you and your brother. Only someone of your superior intelligence and courage could have unraveled the mystery and exposed the true drugstore thief." He paused, then said quietly, "We humbly thank you."

"We knew all along that you weren't the bandit, but I never thought it was Miss Eva either," I confessed. "Anyway, everybody's happy now. Sidney forgave her and she'll be Jack's purple-haired wife next week."

"Nonetheless you exhibited great kindness without thought of reward," the Professor sniffed as he dabbed at his eyes with a big red hanky.

Becoming a bit fidgety, I decided to give him the gift I'd brought. I held it out and said, "This is for you and the Princess. It's a sampler* I embroidered. The little dark spots are blood stains from my needle-pricked fingers."

Taking the framed piece of needlework, he studied it. The Bible verse, surrounded by several, tangle-threaded daisies, read, "Lie not one to another. Col. 3:9." I hoped he'd heed that verse.

The Professor looked down for the longest time. When he raised his head, I noticed tears trickling down his cheeks. He mumbled, simply for a change, "I've never felt so near to God."

I stood on one foot, then the other, then I blurted out "Goodbye" and took off. I didn't pause till I'd flopped down on a sun-soaked rock beside the Muddy Creek bridge.

I'd forgotten to tell the Princess good-bye. But wild horses couldn't drag me back. Good-byes always squeezed my heart till it ached. And I still had Abby's departure to get through.

I plunked rocks into the water and watched the minnows gather to investigate. Then I froze as a butterfly lit on a yarrow weed. I considered stripping the yarrow plant of its bitter smelling flowers for Mama's medicine chest. But I changed my mind when I remembered I might be the one needing the awful tonic for a cold.

I sank back against my rock throne. The hot sun was inviting all my buried freckles to pop out. I'd look a sight, but I didn't care.

I was thinking long thoughts, when Tommy

peeked over the side of the bridge and yelled. "Susie, hurry up! Everybody's frantic. The stage is almost ready to leave with Abby and we couldn't find you."

As I scrambled up the bank, Tommy reached down and grabbed my hand and yanked me to the bridge planking.

"How was I to know the time? I still don't have a watch and it looks like I never will."

Tommy sprinted off toward town. I sped along behind him. We puffed up to the crowd gathered on the front porch of the Grande Hotel. All heads were bowed as Papa asked God to bless Abby in her travels.

As soon as he'd said "Amen," I pushed my way through the elbows and billowing skirts in time to see the men from the Overland Stage lift Abby's trunk to the luggage rack on the top of the stage.

Abby, standing by the stage step, wiped her eyes and tried to smile. Mrs. Higgins hugged her and cautioned, "Land to goodness, you be careful in that big city. City folks aren't to be trusted."

"Oh, Susie," she squealed when she spied me over Mrs. Higgins' pudgy shoulder. She released herself and grabbed me in a bear hug. "I'm going to miss my lively little sister. Do write and remember to pray for me in Chicago."

"I will," I promised while burying my nose into the collar of her lilac-scented traveling suit.

Our farewell was interrupted by a deep voice yelling, "Everybody going with me, better get in. I've a schedule to meet, ya know." After announcing that, the driver spit between his feet and pulled himself up to his high seat.

Abby hastily squeezed every family member. Then Papa helped her up the steps and into the stage.

Someone closed the door, the driver cracked his whip over the horses' heads, and the stage rolled down Horseshoe Bend's Main Street. It picked up speed as it crossed the bridge to the world beyond town.

I watched till I could no longer see the flutter of Abby's hanky, then I fled to my bedroom. By the time I'd used up all my tears, I heard homey sounds coming from my family downstairs.

I shuffled to the commode* and bathed my flushed face with cold water. Then I combed my hair and went downstairs to the kitchen. The aroma puffing from the pots on the stove reminded me that I'd gone without breakfast.

Mama looked up from slicing bread and said, "Susie, your friends, the hair tonic salesman and his wife, stopped by while you were gone and left you that box sitting on the floor. I'm afraid we were so taken up with Abby's leaving that we didn't inquire much about it."

Before I had a chance to get the box open, Aunt Minnie bellowed, "Dinner be served."

But Papa told me to go ahead and open the box before we sat down for the blessing.

The six Conroys that the parsonage still housed gathered around me as I broke the string and lifted the box's flaps. My heat sank. It was crammed full of those familiar green bottles of hair restorer tonic.

Tommy grabbed a bottle and moaned, "He gave you another box of that no-good hair tonic."

"Well now," Aunt Minnie said, "I 'spects he intended for it to be 'bread upon the water,' in return for being so nice to him, you see."

"I suppose," I mumbled as I wondered what I'd do with two boxes of hair tonic.

"Hey, looky!" Joe yelled. "There's a little white package in the corner."

Sure enough, something wrapped in white paper was wedged in one corner of the box. I crouched down and carefully picked it up. The Princess' watch slipped out from the white paper and landed in my lap.

"Wow!" I cried in surprise.

"Oh my!" Mama gasped. "What a lovely watch."

Tommy leaned over my shoulder and remarked, "That's just what Susie's been wanting."

"Sure and it's past believing," Papa added.

"How kindhearted of them," Mama said as she patted my shoulder.

"Faith and if that watch don't be the 'buttered bread,' Susie," Aunt Minnie exclaimed. "And it's me that's been telling you that God always sends 'buttered bread' when we give out plain."

"You sure did," Joe agreed.

For once I was speechless. The only thing my mouth could do was turn up at the corners, while Mama pulled me to my feet and pinned that exquisite, gold watch to the shoulder of my faded everyday calico.

The minute the watch was clasped, I dashed over to look in the mirror. *Sure enough,* I thought as I admired the effect, *the booklet was right.* A dainty, lady's watch dresses up the oldest calico.

Life in 1898

BALM OF GILEAD: An ointment, from a small tree, used for healing. This "balm" probably came from or could be obtained in the biblical town of Gilead. It was the Professor's fancy way of saying Aunt Minnie's soup would help heal the Princess.

CAMERA: By 1898, cameras were fairly common. Tommy's camera outfit was patterned after one offered for $4.25 in Sears, Roebuck, and Company's 1897 catalog. To make it possible for him to develop the picture of the thief in the drugstore (had the scheme worked) his camera used dry plates. (Cameras loaded with film to be developed at the factory were popular also.) Using the photosensitive paper and proper chemicals, furnished with the camera, the glass plates were developed and printed in the home darkroom. The *FLASH LAMP* was a dangerous article offered in the same catalog. Pulling a trigger lighted a "common parlor match" which in turn ignited the explosive powder in the flash pan. The result: a sudden bright light, and maybe, singed eyebrows.

COMMODE: A washstand usually found in bedrooms before the days of indoor plumbing.

FOREHEAD: The Professor's studying the shape of Tommy's forehead, to find out what he was like, was called the "science of phrenology." Modern science has proved that the brain cannot be felt through the bones of the skull.

GODEY'S LADY'S BOOK: A popular magazine of the 19th century picturing, among other things, the latest fashions in clothing.

HANKY: Another word for handkerchief. Tissues were unknown in those days. The sign of a well-dressed man was a clean white handkerchief in his coat pocket. Women carried lacy, or tatted, hankies.

HOMEOPATHIC REMEDIES: Drugs used to treat various diseases.

HORSESHOE BEND: You won't find Horseshoe Bend on an Oregon map. But the town is patterned after any number of small towns in the high desert country of northeastern Oregon.

IRISH: Since Susie's papa (children seldom called their fathers "daddy" then) and aunt Minnie are Irish, it shows up in their speech and conduct. Most of the Conroys seem to have inherited their red hair and impulsive, noisy ways from Papa's side of the family.

LADY'S WATCH: In 1898, wristwatches were not used. Men carried pocket watches and ladies pinned theirs to the shoulders of their dresses. Most of the watch faces were protected by lavishly designed, hinged covers.

LITTLE HOUSE OUT BACK: Before houses had indoor plumbing, these were used in place of bathrooms.

LUMBAGO: Old-time term for a pain in the lower back.

MANGE: A skin disease which causes the hair to fall out. This is usually found in animals.

PARSONAGE: The house, usually on church property, where the preacher lived. Some churches still have parsonages for their pastor. Another word for parsonage is *manse.*

PATE: The top of the head.

POLECAT: Another name for a skunk, which, as you know, isn't known for its pleasant odor.

PORCUPINE: A clumsy, pug-nosed, quill-covered animal. Contrary to popular belief, they can't throw their quills. However, the quills do leave the porcupine at a touch and work their way into the flesh to stay attached like a fishhook.

SALES PITCH or SPIEL: Flowery talk used to persuade someone to buy something. Unfortunately, the truth was (and is) often "stretched" in order to convince the person of how necessary it was that they purchase the item. Let's hope the Professor learned to obey God's words, "Lie not one to another."

SAMPLER: A piece of cloth with a motto or Bible verse embroidered or cross-stitched on it. This was a common way to teach young girls the art of needlework, as well as the truth of the stitched words. Samplers were usually framed and hung when completed.

SHENANIGANS: Irish word for pranks or tricks or mischievous behavior.

SIBLING: A brother or sister.

TATTING: A lace made by looping and knotting heavy thread. In times past, tatting was often attached to the edges of hankies or pillow slips as a decoration.

THUNDER: Thunder is the sound that follows a flash of lightning. The thunder will be heard 6 seconds per mile behind the flash of light, since sound travels slower than light. If a person counts from the time they see the lightning strike till they hear the thunder, they can, more or less, figure the distance to the lightning. Since Susie got to two in her counting, the lightning was about ⅓ of a mile away.

UNCTIONS: Soothing, healing salves.

See what happens when Susie Conroy meets a shifty-eyed bicycle salesman in

The Mystery Man of Horseshoe Bend

And read about Susie's first romance in

The Giant Trunk Mystery